SAVING HIS
MATE

A CRESCENT MOON STORY

Savannah Stuart

Cover art: Jaycee of Sweet 'N Spicy Designs
Author website: www.savannahstuartauthor.com

Publisher's Note: This is a work of fiction. Names, characters, places, and incidents are either the products of the author's imagination or used fictitiously, and any resemblance to actual persons, living or dead, or business establishments, organizations or locales is completely coincidental.

Saving His Mate/KR Press, LLC -- 1st ed.

ISBN-10: 1942447116
ISBN-13: 9781942447115

eISBN: 9780996087414

CHAPTER ONE

"You look like a hobo," Grant said to Rex, eyeing him with clear disgust.

"At least I don't smell like one," he muttered, shifting against the chair in the alpha wolf's office.

Grant snorted. "That's up for debate."

Rex shrugged, not caring that he looked like he'd come straight from a low rent biker bar after getting in a fight with twenty bikers who deserved a good ass-kicking. Because that's exactly where he'd come from. As a 250-year old vampire he needed to let out his aggression sometimes. He preferred sex—though it had been a while—but fighting worked just as well. "Fucking sue me."

The alpha snorted again. "You sound so human when you say that."

He laughed. Vamps and shifters didn't engage in legal battles often. They usually settled things much more violently.

"So what's going on? If I didn't know better, I'd say you're trying to move on my territory."

There wasn't an edge to the male's voice so Rex knew he wasn't being serious.

The truth was, vampires didn't spend much time in shifter territory but over the last year Rex had ended up in Gulf Shores, Alabama multiple times because he'd been hunting rogue vamps, putting him directly into Kincaid pack territory. "Just another job. Foolish newborn robbed a powerful vamp and now I'm hunting him down." And he was getting tired of doing the same thing over and over. For years he'd loved being a bounty hunter. Unlike other powerful, older vamps he'd never been able to put down roots with a coven. He hadn't wanted to. It was odd but he felt more kinship with the wolf sitting across from him than most of his own kind. Wolves and other shifters weren't cold or indifferent to the world like so many vamps.

Grant watched him for a long moment. "You sound exhausted."

Rex half-smiled, not surprised by the other male's observation. He started to respond when the door behind him opened. Before he turned he scented two females, one who was Talia, Grant's human-mate-turned-shifter. He shifted in his seat and stood as the women entered. He nodded politely at both of them and waited until they'd entered before he sat back down. It didn't matter how old he was, certain manners had been bred into him hundreds of years ago. Turned at the beginning of the American Revolution, to say he was from a different generation would be an understatement.

"Hey, Rex," Talia said, hurrying to her mate. She practically jumped in Grant's lap, wrapping her arms around his neck as she planted a noisy kiss on his cheek.

From the subtle scent of vodka wafting off her and the other female he vaguely recognized, he guessed they'd been drinking. And it was clear Talia wanted to be alone with her mate.

Rex stood. "Grant, I won't be in town longer than I have to be. Thanks for letting me hunt in your territory."

Keeping his arm wrapped around Talia's waist as he held her in his lap, the male shook his head slightly. "I don't care how long you're here... And I'd like to talk to you about taking a permanent position with my pack. It'd mean no more bounty hunting except jobs I might need. But you could put down roots if you want to."

The alpha couldn't have shocked Rex more if he'd tried. Rex frowned, watching Grant as the other female sat in the chair he'd vacated with a sigh of exhaustion.

"Oh, a vampire in our pack! We'll be like the United Nations of packs. Wolf and jaguar shifters and now a vampire. I like it," the female said, her words slightly slurred. She wasn't being insincere either, even if she was clearly intoxicated. Sarah; that was her name. He recognized her from a BDSM club where he'd been hunting a rogue. She'd been whipping some guy with a flogger. Definitely not his scene.

He ignored her and narrowed his gaze at Grant. He knew the alpha wouldn't have made the offer if he wasn't serious. Grant wouldn't joke about something like that. "We'll discuss this tomorrow. Alone."

Grant grinned, as if he thought he knew Rex's answer. How could Grant when Rex didn't know—even if he was tempted. "Meet me at the house after dark."

"I'll be there." He nodded once at Talia and started to turn toward the door when a subtle lavender scent rolled over him. His fangs ached at the sight of a tall, leggy female shifter standing in the doorway. With beautifully bronzed skin and a knee-length black dress that hugged her slender body in all the right places, his mouth practically watered as he drank in all her subtle curves. The dress tied around the back of her neck in a halter style and the way it pulled against her breasts showed enough cleavage that he felt like...hell, he'd never felt like this. For how slender she was, her breasts were surprisingly full. More than a handful and right about now, he could easily envision cupping them, licking them, teasing...

The dark-haired woman flicked a glance at him for a millisecond before looking right past him. He couldn't stop staring if his life depended on it and she'd barely noticed him. Talk about a blow to his ego.

"Are you two hooligans done for the night?" the beautiful woman asked.

Rex stared, his gaze tracking her as she moved farther into the room. His heart rate kicked up a notch and he had to force it to remain steady, to appear as if he was unaffected. Unlike the human myths that said vamps didn't have hearts, he definitely did. And right now his was beating out of control. What the hell was wrong with him? His fangs pushed at his gums, aching to be unleashed with an insistency he hadn't felt in over two centuries. It was...

Fuck.

No. No, no, no.

It was *not* what he thought it was. He refused to even think the words.

"You can't use a word like hooligan. You sound like an eighty year old woman," Talia teased, still perched in Grant's lap, though she swayed slightly and Rex realized she'd had more to drink than he originally thought.

"I'm two hundred," the female said, laughter in her voice. "Grant, these two maniacs are done for the night. I'm sure you'll get Talia home so I'm taking Sarah back to the compound."

The compound was the condominium complex the pack owned. Pricey beach front property where every packmate had a view of the ocean. It was right next to Grant's two-story beach house. Seriously prime real estate.

"Hey, I don't need...yeah, okay maybe I do," Sarah slurred again, slumping against the chair.

"I'll escort them," Rex blurted, surprising himself and everyone else in the room.

All eyes turned his way and he could feel Grant's curious gaze on him but Rex just watched the dark-haired female. Her espresso-colored gaze raked over him from head to toe, as if she found his offer amusing. She raised an eyebrow then turned back to her alpha without even acknowledging him. "I've got Sarah."

Grant nodded. "Okay, but Rex will go with you, Margery."

The female stilled, her jaw tightening. "I don't need any help taking a drunk packmate home. Especially not from a vampire."

What the hell did that mean? Rex frowned, but didn't respond. Maybe she didn't trust vampires. That wouldn't be out of the realm of possibilities. Just because he and Grant were friends didn't mean that vamp-shifter friendships were normal.

"I'm not drunk," Sarah muttered as she fiddled with her cell phone. It appeared as if she was trying to unlock the screen but couldn't figure out her code.

"Humor me." There was no give to Grant's voice, his wolf in his eyes as he gave her an order.

"Grant." She gave her alpha an imploring look and for some reason Rex was positive there was more to her hesitancy than she was saying aloud. Margery and Grant were clearly having an unspoken conversation. After a long moment, the female sighed. "Fine, but no baked goods for you for a month," she snapped in annoyance.

To Rex's surprise, Grant just grinned again while Talia loudly whispered that she'd share her stash with him.

As Margery helped Sarah to her feet, she muttered something under her breath about obnoxious vampires. Moving into action, Rex went to help her, but she shot him an annoyed glare so he backed off.

"I don't need your help," she said quietly.

"My name is Rex." It wasn't exactly hostility he sensed in her voice, but she was definitely wary of his kind. He didn't like it. For some reason the thought of this female feeling anything for him other than hunger raked against his senses like silver daggers.

She didn't respond, just steadied her packmate and headed for the door. Rex wasn't sure why Grant had ordered the female to let him help, but he wasn't going to question the alpha. The woman—Margery—had the most addicting scent. It wasn't just her natural lavender scent, there was something else under the surface driving his senses crazy. As he started to shut the door behind them he saw Talia straddling Grant and quickly pulled it closed.

As they reached the elevators, Sarah swayed against Margery and Rex immediately reached out a hand to help steady her. If his fingers happened to brush against Margery's shoulder then all the better for him.

She instantly pulled away from him in the elevator, putting intentional distance between them as she pressed the button for one of the parking garages. And she was still avoiding his gaze.

"Grant asked him to join our pack," Sarah said in what she probably thought was a whisper as she laid her head on Margery's shoulder. "He's cute." Even if she had been whispering he still would have heard her with his supernatural hearing. Something the female had likely forgotten in her inebriated state.

Margery looked at him then, full-on this time, not just a glance. Her dark eyes were so damn captivating he couldn't have looked away if he'd wanted to. "You're Rex the bounty hunter? The one who helped Ella with that vampire back in January?"

He nodded, hoping that would give him some standing with her when clearly she didn't like vampires. He probably wasn't helping his cause when he looked beat to hell in grungy jeans, shit-kickers and a ripped T-shirt. "Yes. And normally I don't smell like dirty humans. I got into an altercation earlier this evening."

"You think humans are dirty?"

"No, but the ones I fought were." The stench of booze and sex had been rolling off them in pungent waves.

She relaxed a fraction at his words, which told him she clearly liked humans. Made sense considering her alpha had mated one. "Are you the same Rex who took Talia out on a date?"

He froze at her question. The elevator jerked to a halt, the soft ding alerting them they were at their destination.

She didn't wait for a response, just muttered under her breath again as she exited the elevator with Sarah.

Rex was right on her heels. "It was one time and before I knew she was with Grant." It wasn't as if they'd even kissed. He'd asked the pretty human out because he'd thought she was available. He hadn't known she'd been in a fight with her then-boyfriend—or that her boyfriend had been a powerful alpha. Hell, Grant hadn't even told her about the existence of supernatural beings at the time.

"Hmm," was all she said as she retrieved a keyfob from her small purse. She pressed one of the buttons and a nearby Jeep beeped. "You don't need to escort us any further, vampire."

"My name is Rex and I'm going with you." He gritted his teeth at her tone and her use of the word vampire instead of his name. "Is it all vampires or just me in particular you have a problem with?"

At his question guilt flickered in her dark, mesmerizing gaze. "I'm...sorry. I'm not normally such a bitch," she muttered.

"It's true, Margery's so sweet. She's like the mom of our pack," Sarah murmured, snuggling closer to her packmate. "She just needs to get laid."

Rex's eyes widened and Margery's bronze face flamed crimson as she continued. "I've had a stressful day and it's not personal, I swear. I'm sorry for being rude, but I really don't need you to follow us back to the compound."

"I'm not going to follow you." She relaxed until he continued. "I'm riding with you." And he wasn't letting the female out of his sight until she was safely back at the compound. Something about her had all his possessive, protective instincts flaring to life. There was no way in hell he'd fight this feeling. Not when he knew what it could mean.

CHAPTER TWO

Margery resisted the urge to fidget or show any signs that she was uncomfortable having a vampire sitting in the backseat of her Jeep. Sarah was sitting in the front next to her, lightly snoring. She'd passed out before they'd left the parking garage.

She hated that she felt the oddest attraction to Rex. It was making her wolf claw at her insides, wanting to strut around and preen for the male. And that was not like her. Especially not for a vampire. After what had happened to her as a cub she'd never gotten over her distrust of his kind. Something Grant very well knew. Which just infuriated her. It also told her that her alpha must trust this vampire a lot to send him with her.

Because he knew that she didn't need an escort. She was a strong, capable shifter. Not that weak, defenseless cub.

"I'm surprised I haven't seen you around over the last year," Rex said from the backseat.

She resisted the urge to look at him in the rear-view mirror as she pulled up to a stoplight. The man was too sexy for his own good. Even disheveled and dirty, it would be impossible to hide all that masculine appeal. Tall, muscular with dark blond hair cut close to his head. She didn't even normally go for blonds. Of course she never went for vampires either. Hell, maybe Sarah was right and she did need to get laid. It was the only explanation for the weird restless sensation humming through her with Rex near. Her wolf was urging her to do all sorts of naughty things to the male, taking her by surprise. She'd been in control of her wolf since she was a cub, but now she felt jittery and edgy.

Realizing she needed to respond, she shrugged. "We've got a big pack. I'm sure you haven't met a lot of us."

"How long have you been with Grant's pack?"

That was a safe enough question. "A long time. His father was my alpha."

Rex snorted at that, taking her by surprise. She glanced at him in the mirror to find him watching her with those dark hazel eyes. They were almost a chocolate color, but not quite. There was the slightest hint of green in them and the effect was startling in the dim interior of her Jeep. The soft glow of his vampire eyes let her know he was feeling *something* for her right now too. She didn't know from personal experience but she'd heard that vampires' eyes glowed when they were turned on.

"You didn't like his father?"

"The male was an archaic monster. It's amazing Grant is the way he is," Rex said.

Agreeing with his assessment, Margery settled back against her seat, relaxing more, and belatedly realized she'd been hunched over and gripping the steering wheel for dear life. She had to get a hold of herself. She wasn't an inexperienced young cub unable to protect herself. Her human and wolf side were warring with each other and it was beyond stressful. Her human side was fighting fear while her wolf side wanted to punch her fear in the face and rub her body all over Rex. Seriously, what the heck? She wasn't a feline in heat.

She lightly cleared her throat as she continued driving. "I agree. His father wasn't exactly a monster, but was very mistrustful of outsiders. Anyone who wasn't part of the pack." And Grant definitely wasn't like that. The world was changing and he was taking big strides in the shifter community.

He'd mated with a human and now had jaguar shifters living with them.

"What do you do for the pack?"

"What do you mean?" she asked, slowing as she reached the turn-off for the condo entrance located right off Beach Boulevard. She typed in the access code, not bothering to check if Rex watched her. He was a vampire and if he wanted inside their complex, he could just scale the wall surrounding the private parking lot in one jump. Of course he'd be tackled by one of her many packmates, but the privacy gate was for humans, not supernatural beings.

"Your packmate insinuated that you were like a mother to the pack. Do you have...cubs?"

"No. And I'm just one of the oldest members, that's probably why she said that." Only it wasn't. Margery was one of the caretaker figures of the pack, definitely a mother figure. But right now her wolf didn't want Rex thinking of her in those terms. She wanted him thinking of her as a sensual, desirable female. Which just frustrated her even more. She should not want this male and she definitely shouldn't care what he thought. It was a miracle she'd managed to suppress the scent of her need as long as she had. She had to get away from Rex before he realized the effect he was having on her body. Because she had no doubt he'd use it against her.

"I run a bakery near the casino," she told him, surprising herself. She shouldn't be giving him information and inviting conversation. Damn it, she couldn't seem to stop herself.

"Margery's Bakery? That's *you*. I've heard a lot of good things about it from the supernatural community. I always thought the way you keep your hours was smart."

It was silly, but she actually blushed at his words. At least the interior was dark enough that he wouldn't be able to tell. She opened her bakery right after sunset and kept it open until ten in the morning. She got the supernatural community, the casino crowds leaving early in the morning and during spring break and summer months, she snagged tons of business. Considering most of the pack kept night hours it was perfect for her schedule. "Thanks."

As she pulled into one of the empty parking spots Rex cleared his throat almost nervously. "Would you like to go on a date one evening this week?"

The sweet way he asked took her off guard as much as the question. "Ah, thank you but I'm going to pass." She was damn well going to force her wolf into submission. Before he could respond she'd unstrapped her seatbelt and was out of the Jeep. By the time she'd rounded the vehicle to Sarah's side, Rex was out and leaning against the passenger door—effectively blocking Margery from helping her sleeping packmate out.

There was a gleam in his eyes she couldn't define as he watched her. Even though she was tall, she had to tip her head back to look at him. His crisp, earthy scent was driving her crazy. "Are you saying no because I'm a vampire? Because I can scent your desire. I didn't at first, but I can now. Clearly." There was a sexy edge to his words that sent a shiver down her spine. And his expression was so full of wicked promises it was all she could do not to melt into him.

She flushed at his words, not bothering to deny what she felt. But it didn't matter what her wolf wanted. She wrapped her arms around herself, then realized it pushed her breasts up more. Quickly she dropped them when his gaze strayed to her cleavage, his eyes softly glowing. "Yes, it's because you're a vampire and before you push me..."

She took a deep breath, getting ready to tell him something she almost never talked about. But with the way he was clearly ready to pursue her, she knew she needed to give him a solid reason to back off. Dominant males in the supernatural world were like that. "When I was a cub, about sixteen, I was ambushed by four vampires. The world was different then." 1814 had been utter chaos, with British soldiers having just burned down the White House. "I think you're older than me so I'm sure you remember. Long story short, I was packless at the time and unprotected. They would have gang-raped me if I hadn't shifted to my wolf. Since they couldn't carry out what they intended, they decided to nearly beat me to death instead. So, I don't date vampires."

He didn't respond, just sucked in a sharp breath as she nudged him out of the way. With shaking hands she managed to rouse Sarah enough to help her out of the vehicle. Margery didn't bother looking back at Rex as she walked Sarah up to the complex. She knew her words would have made everything clear to him and that he wouldn't bother pursuing her.

Margery knew it was stupid to let something from her youth affect her so many years later, but some things were imprinted on your psyche, especially things that happened when you were young. It didn't matter that her wolf wanted him, her human side felt too vulnerable around vampires and that was never going to change. She'd never really cared about that. Until now. Rex brought up the strangest sensation in her that her wolf didn't want to deny. And if she was being honest, the most feminine part of her didn't want to deny either.

* * *

Rex watched Margery walk away, using all his willpower to restrain himself from going after her. Her words had been like silver knives clawing over his bare skin. Trying to talk to her now wouldn't do any good. What could he say? *Don't blame me for something four monsters did.* No. He needed to *show* her that he was different.

The thought of her vulnerable, injured...fuck. It sliced him up, the need to destroy whoever had hurt her building up inside him with a surprising vengeance. This type of protectiveness was new, but he embraced it. Even if he didn't quite understand it. Once she was safely within the confines of the complex, he turned and headed for the gate. He scented a couple shifters nearby but didn't bother asking anyone to open the gate for him.

He jumped it, then glanced around. Whereas the casino was perpetually busy, there weren't any humans out near the complex around this time of night. And he had just a few hours left before sunrise to find that rogue youth he'd been hunting. He already had a lead on the male and would have gone after him directly after speaking to Grant, but the need to be near Margery had been overwhelming.

And still was.

Using his gift of speed, he raced back to the casino where he'd left his SUV. Normally he preferred his bike, but when bounty hunting, he always took his SUV. The back section was soundproofed and he'd made it into a virtual prison for transporting vampires. If anyone opened the hatch they'd see a silver-lined, impenetrable box. The headrest was a cotton pillow. He might be bringing them back for sentencing but he wasn't cruel. He had his prisoners dress in clothing that covered their entire bodies to protect them from the silver and the box was big enough that they had space to be semi-comfortable. But the silver interior guaranteed they wouldn't be able to escape.

The drive to his destination near the main highway was quicker than he'd expected, but it was late and most people in Gulf Shores stayed near the beach. The place he was heading to was strictly a paranormal hangout. Just a bed and breakfast owned by a vampire—that Grant knew about since it was technically in his territory—that supernatural beings stayed at when they were passing through. It wasn't as if they advertised, but the supernatural community talked and Rex had tailed more than one rogue vamp from this place. As he turned down a quiet, dusty makeshift-road lined with a cow pasture on one side and a pecan tree orchard on the other, he rolled down his window a fraction and listened intently.

Once he reached the end of the road, he pulled off onto a grassy patch near the fence on the cow pasture side and slipped out. He'd disabled his dome light, but he was still preternaturally quiet.

Moving with a burst of supernatural speed, he raced down the rest of the dusty road until he reached a small, white gate and fence surrounding a two-story brick home. Without pause he jumped the small, three-foot gate and only stopped once he was on the front of the wraparound porch.

Pressing his back against the brick wall near the front door, he listened and could hear four distinct voices inside. One female—Charmaine, the owner—and three males. Rex instantly recognized Stanley's arrogant voice from a video he'd watched. The vampire who Stanley had stolen from had taken the youth in and given him a place to live, tried to teach him a work ethic, but the foolish male had stolen from his new leader instead and run. Soon he would pay for his crimes.

After circling the home and checking the outlying areas for any more supernatural beings, Rex returned to the front door. It would be sunrise soon enough and he was tired of this hunt so he decided to go for the direct approach. Instead of storming in and destroying Charmaine's home, he knocked on the front door.

Everything went silent so he called out, "Charmaine, make yourself scarce. Stanley, come outside and make this easy on yourself. You can't run forever."

For one long moment silence reigned but then there was a flurry of movement inside. Rex heard Charmaine mutter *dumbass* before there was a crash and breaking of glass from the back of the house.

On another burst of speed, Rex rounded the house and raced after the vampire dashing across the land behind the house. The nearly full moon and stars above gave him plenty of guidance, though he didn't need it with his night vision.

Charmaine owned this pecan orchard but it wouldn't give enough cover for the rogue vamp to hide for long.

As Stanley neared a big pecan tree he looked over his shoulder and brought something up in his hand.

A gun.

The sight of it enraged Rex, his vision going red. How pathetic, using a modern weapon. He dodged to the right as a bullet whizzed past his head. It made a soft sound as it embedded in a tree trunk. Using the trees as cover, he followed the obnoxiously loud—clearly untrained vamp—by sound alone.

"I don't want to hurt you, man!" Stanley shouted.

Rex measured the distance using his senses. Maybe fifty yards to his right. He flew past three giant trees spread out evenly in the orchard, closing in. Only twenty five yards to go now.

"Listen, I'm sorry. We can work this out. I'll cut you in on what I took." Stanley's voice was whiny and shaky now.

Even more pathetic. *First he actually shoots at me, then tries to bribe me.* Whoever had turned Stanley should be staked. Vampires used to be more discerning when they turned a human.

Rex headed in the direction Stanley had called out from, slowing when he neared a huge pecan tree on the very edge of the orchard. He knew Stanley thought he had the upper hand, but Rex could scent him.

Feigning that he was looking around, he used all the strength in his legs and jumped high into the air in a fluid movement. Stanley's eyes widened as Rex landed on the branch next to him. The rogue started to raise his weapon-wielding hand but Rex grabbed his wrist and squeezed, breaking Stanley's bones. The gun fell from his fingers as he screamed, tumbling to the grassy earth below.

"Didn't anyone ever teach you that stealing was wrong?" Rex asked as he wrapped his fingers around Stanley's neck. He squeezed tight, making his point clear; *try to run and I'll rip your head off.* He didn't need to say the words for the dumbass to understand. "We're going to jump down then head back to my SUV. Then you're going to come with me and pay back all the money you stole." And likely be tortured for a while, but that wasn't Rex's business.

Stanley's eyes glowed a bright amber as he shook his head. Taking Rex by surprise, he punched out at the branch with his non-broken arm.

Rex went for one of his blades as the branch cracked and broke. Stanley slashed out with his claws, slicing into Rex's forearm as the branch gave way beneath him. So amped up on adrenaline, Rex barely felt the dig into his flesh, but he let the guy go and jumped down as Stanley fell. The vamp's arms flailed as he fell backward.

Rex's feet hit the ground a second before Stanley did, his boots thudding softly. Stanley landed on his back and started to roll over when his eyes suddenly widened, going bright amber before he turned to ash.

What the hell?

Spine tingling, Rex crouched low, backing up toward the tree as he scanned the area for more threats. Using all his senses it took less than ten seconds for him to realize he was alone. A couple cows made groaning sounds about a hundred yards away but there were no people—human or supernatural—in the direct vicinity.

He waited another thirty seconds before moving from the tree and crouching next to the pile of ash. Three sharp branches stuck straight up in the air like blades. One of them must have punctured Stanley's heart.

Talk about an unlucky fall. Shaking his head at the irony of Stanley basically killing himself by trying to escape, he gathered the male's clothes and weapons. He'd send them back to the vamp who'd hired him and receive eighty percent of his payment. Normally he'd be pissed when one of his hunted died because he didn't receive the full payment. Now...he didn't need to leave anytime soon. Which meant he could spend all his time courting Margery.

CHAPTER THREE

Rex tried to appear casual as he sat on Grant's couch, waiting for the alpha to get off the phone with whatever packmate he was talking to. All he wanted to do was go see Margery, but knew he needed to speak with Grant first. There always seemed to be a crisis, which was pretty normal for shifter packs or vampire covens. If he agreed to join Grant's pack—and he couldn't believe that he was actually contemplating it—he figured that was something he'd have to get used to.

As he leaned back against the leather couch, Talia walked into the room smelling like sand and salt. Her hair was damp and her black bathing suit straps were visible. "Hey, Rex. How long have you been here?"

"Just a few minutes."

"He shouldn't be too long." She stood there watching him curiously but didn't say anything.

He shifted against the seat. "Are you working tonight?"

She shook her head. "No. I'm not at the bar anymore anyway."

"Right." He knew that. She'd been in school for marine sciences or something before. She must have finished her Master's degree by now. "What do you do now?"

"Aquarium curator," she said almost absently before continuing. "So, what's up with you and Margery?"

He wasn't taking the bait. "An aquarium curator? That sounds interesting."

She crossed her arms over her chest and flopped down on the couch across from him. "Come on. Sarah said you two were hot for each other. I want details. We haven't had anything exciting happen around here for almost three months."

"I'm surprised Sarah can remember any of last night."

"Oh, she does and she said you two stunk with an overdose of hormones. She also—"

"Talia." Grant sounded mildly annoyed as he strode into the room, phone-free. "I need to talk to Rex. You can stay, but no pack gossip talk."

She let out an over-exaggerated sigh as she stood and brushed her lips over Grant's. "See ya later,

Rex," she tossed over her shoulder as she left the room.

Once she was upstairs and Rex could hear the shower running, Grant finally sat across from him. The room was definitely masculine, with furniture made of leather and sturdy wood. Some of it Rex recognized as being antique and worth a fortune. He could also see Talia's feminine touches. And not just in the décor. He could see it in his friend. The alpha was still tough as hell but he didn't seem as edgy. Or lonely.

"She's good for you," Rex murmured, glad for his friend.

Grant's eyebrows rose a fraction in clear surprise. He nodded, but didn't comment. "Have you given my offer any thought?"

Rex liked that he didn't have to bullshit with the alpha. The male always got straight to the point. "What exactly are you offering, because I'm not a beta." And he never would be. It just wasn't his personality.

Grant snorted. "You think Max and Asher have beta personalities?"

The corners of Rex's mouth lifted. Grant's second-in-command and cousin were definitely not beta males. "No, but...yeah, okay. I get what you're saying." He'd never say it, but Rex believed Asher was strong enough to have his own pack. But from what he knew of the male, he didn't think Asher wanted the responsibility. "So why me? Why a vampire? And...why now?"

Grant leaned forward a fraction, his expression unreadable. "First, I trust you. And the fact that you're a vampire is a plus. As far as the timing..." He paused and Rex could tell he was searching for the right words. The alpha wasn't known for being delicate so he wasn't sure if that was a good or bad thing. Finally he let out a small sigh. "Times are changing. Over the last year we've seen more rogue vampires entering our territory. Their stay is short-lived." He gave a dark smile, his wolf clear in his gaze for a moment. "But sooner or later the shit will hit the fan and the wrong vamp will end up getting killed in my territory. Whether it's a justified kill or not, you know as well as I do that if a coven leader is looking for a war, anything could set it off. But if you're part of my pack and either mete out the kill or support us..." He trailed off, shrugging, letting Rex fill in the rest.

The male's foresight was what made him a good alpha. Rex had never wanted to settle down until recently. About a year ago to be exact. He felt as if he'd been roaming around aimlessly for so damn long, never fitting in anywhere. Certainly not with his own kind. When he'd run into Grant a year ago, it'd been good to see the alpha—even when the male had punched him in the face for taking Talia out. "The thought is surprisingly appealing."

Grant's mouth quirked up in that obnoxious alpha way of his.

"I will not be submissive."

Grant snorted. "I don't want that. You're powerful and a good ally and you'll never be a threat to take over the pack since you're not a shifter. We'll never have a power struggle in the sense that matters to my wolf."

Rex nodded, understanding. He could literally never be alpha of a shifter pack because he was a vampire. No wolves would ever follow him—and it wasn't in his temperament to be a leader of a group anyway. "Would I live within the compound?" He was still trying to wrap his head around the possibility.

"I would prefer you did. There's an empty place right next to Margery's." Grant's voice was deadpan, but Rex knew the mention of the beautiful wolf was intentional. "Wherever you reside, we can make changes so it's suitable for your sleeping needs."

Grant's pack lived and worked vampire hours so it wouldn't be that difficult to fit in with their pack life. "Why did you send me with the females last night?"

The alpha frowned, possibly picking up on the edginess in Rex. "I saw the way you looked at Margery."

Rex gritted his teeth, not liking that he'd been that transparent. But more than that, his presence had distressed Margery and that made him more than edgy. "She was hurt by my kind. You should have told me. If I'd known I'd have never ridden in the backseat. My presence had to have made her feel vulnerable."

Grant's expression didn't change, but his wolf flickered in his gaze. "I didn't think of it like that. Shit." He rubbed a hand over his face. "I'm an idiot. I saw the way you both looked at each other and I thought..." He let out another curse and stood. "I owe her an apology. Wait, she *told* you what happened to her?"

Rex nodded, not moving from his position as Grant sat back down. "Yes." Now the alpha looked truly surprised. Before he could respond, Rex continued. "I'm planning to court her. Is there anyone else in the pack interested in her?" Not that he cared, but he wanted to know if he had competition.

"There are males interested, but none she's interested in. Damn, court her? You're serious."

Rex flicked a gaze upward. "Does your mate eavesdrop?"

"Always, but she won't repeat anything you say here."

Rex decided to be blunt, to trust this male in a way he rarely trusted anyone. If he was going to join this pack—and he was pretty certain he would—he had to open himself up to the alpha. "I think she's my mate. I've never responded to a female like that before. My fangs ached, my—" He cut himself off; Grant didn't need to know everything about his visceral response.

"Her eyes went pure wolf when she saw you. I've never seen her do that before."

Rex hadn't noticed, but she'd barely glanced at him. The revelation was interesting and welcome. "I plan to pursue her hard."

"Good."

One simple word. All Rex needed to hear. He'd be doing it with or without the alpha's approval but he was glad the male knew of his intention. "I will give you an answer soon." But first he had to see if there was a possibility of a future with Margery. He couldn't be in a pack with her if she rejected him. Something primal and raw inside him couldn't bear it if she did. He couldn't be faced with seeing her day in and day out if they had no future.

* * *

Margery pounded the dough against the prep station, wishing it was her irresponsible packmate Sapphire. Okay, Sapphire wasn't actually irresponsible, but she'd promised to help out at the bakery tonight then gotten called back to the Crescent Moon Bar to work. Margery still had Sarah out front assisting the customers, but that meant Margery was stuck in the back baking all night—because there was no way she was letting Sarah take over her kitchen.

That was the one bad thing about being in a pack. Sometimes they got stretched too thin. Max needed the help at the bar and because of his position Sapphire had to help him over Margery.

Margery wanted to fume about that but knew that the truth was, if she'd asked Max, he'd have let Sapphire stay on and he'd have dealt with the mess at the bar. But she was in a mood tonight and felt like mentally berating anyone and everyone.

Sadly, she knew why. Ever since meeting that too-sexy-for-his-own-good vampire she was feeling restless. The kind of restless that made her skin feel too tight for her body and reminded her how long it had been since she'd had sex. Really good, toe-curling sex.

As a two-hundred year old shifter she'd had lovers, but she'd always been careful about picking who she slept with for a multitude of reasons. The main one being that male shifters were so damn territorial. Sometimes they couldn't just take sex for what it was. Simple sex. No, they had to get all alpha and possessive.

It meant she had to go outside her pack or risk some male going all alpha macho on her and getting protective when she didn't need or want it. Since she didn't sleep with humans, finding available male shifters outside her pack had been damn near impossible in the past couple years. She worked too much and what sane shifter would come into Grant's territory? No one, that's who.

She slammed her fist against the dough again then stilled when the whole prep table shook. Crap, she was going to break something if she didn't rein her wolf in. Sighing, she set it aside then froze when she felt an almost electric energy streak through the air.

Like a tangible thing, she felt Rex's presence throughout her entire body, singing all her nerve endings. Seriously, what the hell was going on with her? A vampire shouldn't get her all worked up and needy. She glanced up from her work station when the swinging door to the back kitchen opened, fully expecting Sarah to pop her head in and announce that Rex was here. To her surprise Rex strode in like he owned the place. All sexy, alpha male looking too delicious for his own good.

Wearing a button-down dark green shirt that made his eyes even more gorgeous, and custom-made black pants, he looked different than last night. More polished, but no less primal. No, he was a predator through and through. She saw it in every line of his body and the intense way he was watching her, those beautiful eyes of his missing nothing.

"What are you doing in my kitchen?" she demanded.

"You need help out there." A blunt statement.

"Thank you, Captain Obvious. Now answer the question." She knew she sounded testy and a little bitchy but she couldn't help it. Her hormones were wreaking havoc inside her. Just the sight of him had her wanting to strip them both naked and go at it right on the kitchen floor. Damn her inner wolf.

A ghost of a smile played across those full lips that she wanted to lick and nip. He was probably smug because he could scent her desire. "I'm grabbing an apron," he said as he looked behind the swinging door to where half a dozen clean white aprons with the words 'Margery's Bakery' were printed in red script across the front pocket.

She blinked. "Why?"

He slipped one of the aprons over his head and tied it behind his waist. "Because I'm going to run one of the cash registers for you."

"You can't do that," she sputtered, feeling more out of sorts than ever. What the heck was happening? A vampire was coming in to help her at the bakery?

"It's easy, and I am." Without waiting for a response, he strode from the kitchen, the door swinging in his wake behind him.

Wiping her hands against her apron, she hurried after him. She started to follow through the door but stopped and watched him through the circular glass window. Damn that male for looking so sexy in a freaking apron. The tie was right above his very tight, delectable butt. Clothes simply couldn't hide the muscular body of that male. And he was doing a fine job helping customers, moving with an efficiency that almost belied his supernatural speed. But not quite.

When she saw that the two lines were almost to the door, she decided to let him help her out. She needed it and there was no reason she shouldn't accept his assistance. As long as he didn't think she owed him anything for it, they'd be fine.

Hours later and close to ten there was a lull in business—yet she was still hiding out in the kitchen like a big coward. Rex and Sarah had both been back a few times to grab trays of pastries, cupcakes, muffins and pretty much everything she'd been busting her ass making. With the exception of his smoldering looks, Rex hadn't said much to her. The male didn't need to. Not when he was telling her exactly what he wanted to do with her with just his eyes. For some reason that didn't bother her at all. Just the opposite. With her history with vamps she'd assumed she'd never find one attractive. Now she found this male more attractive than any male, regardless of species. It was maddening.

She tensed when the swinging door opened up but instantly relaxed when Sarah strode in. "Hey, boss."

"Hey. You doing okay out there?"

"Yeah. It's quiet so I'm taking a smoke break."

Margery frowned. "You don't smoke."

Sarah snorted. "Fine, I'm staying back here until you go talk to that gorgeous vampire. If you don't make a move, I will."

Margery's claws extended at the thought of her packmate going after Rex. To her annoyance Sarah just laughed.

"You're so easy," she muttered, heading for one of the walk-in coolers, chuckling under her breath.

Taking a deep breath, Margery willed her claws back in and decided to stop being such a coward. As she pushed open the swinging door she nearly slammed into Rex who was coming back into the kitchen. They both paused, watching each other. Shifters had a higher body temperature than vamps and humans but right now his body heat might as well be a freaking volcano. With him so close and that addictive scent teasing her, it took all her self-control not to lean into him and take what she wanted.

Her mouth felt as if it was filled with cotton but she figured she should be the first to speak, especially since he'd been nice enough to help. Not that she thought his intentions were noble. He clearly wanted to get into her pants.

And her wolf clearly wanted him in them. If she was being honest with herself, she did too.

She fidgeted with the front of her apron, hating that she was so rumpled. "Thanks for helping out with the early crowd."

His gaze flicked to her mouth as she spoke, those dark hazel eyes of his glowing for a moment. Taking her by surprise, he reached out and cupped her cheek and jaw in his powerful hand. She was too stunned to pull away and when he swiped his thumb across her bottom lip her nipples actually tightened.

"You have a little icing here," he murmured, his voice pure seduction. Like the richest, most decadent piece of chocolate cake.

"Thanks." When she was stressed she tended to eat. If it wasn't for her crazy high shifter metabolism she probably wouldn't eat so much, but her nerves were frayed so she'd been snacking like a rabid wolf. On instinct she flicked her tongue out, moistening her bottom lip. She could almost taste him, knew he'd be dark and spicy.

Rex groaned as he dropped his hand, his gaze never wavering. "Are you working all night?"

She nodded, struggling to find her voice again.

"I'm sorry about making you feel vulnerable last night."

His words were like ice water splashing her in the face. She stepped out from their intimate enclosure in the doorway and into the shop. "You didn't." Out of instinct she glanced around but the place had cleared out. For now. She knew in another hour or so it would fill up again and they'd be busy for at least two more hours after that until the normal morning rush. Business always came in spurts like that. Not that she was really focused on any of that now.

To give herself something to do, she went to one of the cash registers and typed in her code to run the current report. Yeah, because right now her mind was totally on sales. Rex was practically glued to her as he followed, though he wasn't actually touching her. He leaned against the glass counter, inches from her; a demanding presence that refused to be ignored. She wanted to smack him or kiss him, she couldn't decide.

"Then I'm sorry we got off on the wrong foot. I would like to make it up to you." His darkly delicious voice rolled over her, making other parts of her tingle. The male was a menace.

"That's not necessary." Her words came out all high-pitched, like some nervous cub.

"I think it's very necessary." The seductive note in his voice made her glance at him.

Immediately she wished she hadn't. Her gaze zeroed in on his lips and damn him, he gave her a disarming half-smile because he clearly knew the affect he was having on her body. "What do you want from me?" The question came out as a whisper.

"You really want me to spell it out?" He cupped her cheek again, but this time she could feel the strength and dominance thrumming through him, an out of control beat that made her entire body tingle in an erotic awareness. Just imagining what he would do to her, how he'd touch her—and how she could touch him made her overheat with need.

She swallowed hard and tried to tell herself to pull back from him. She should...for some reason. But she couldn't make her body respond to the mental command. Feeling almost possessed she leaned closer to him, inhaling his addictive scent as she fantasized what it would be like to kiss him.

Even last night when he'd smelled like sweaty humans there'd been an underlying earthy smell. Not in the way that shifters scented, but more crisp—and no less erotic for it. It made her wolf crazy for this male in a way she'd never experienced.

The bell attached to the front door jingled and she practically jumped back from Rex. His strong jaw tightened in annoyance, but she turned away, ready to greet a customer. She smiled when she saw Davis, one of her packmates. He was a perfect buffer and she desperately needed one.

"Hey, Davis. What are you doing here? I thought you were at the casino helping with security." He worked with Asher, Grant's cousin, at the casino the pack owned. Though he was in his fifties, he looked like he was in his mid-twenties. Over six feet tall, he was muscular and intimidating looking—and he had the fighting skills to back up his appearance.

Davis barely glanced at her, instead focusing on Rex who was hovering a scant foot from her. "Max said you might need some help. What are you doing in town, Rex?" The question was benign enough but there was an underlying edge to it. Which surprised her. Davis was dominant in nature and had fought Asher in the way wolves did to prove who was stronger—and lost—when the other wolf had joined their pack months ago. But for the most part he was even-tempered. It was why he was so good with the security team.

"Bounty-hunting." Rex's short answer sounded just as strained as Davis. As if he was controlling his need to fight.

Her packmate moved toward them, winding his way through the round, high-top tables. "Shouldn't you be out hunting then." Not exactly a question.

"Job's over and Grant asked me to join the pack."

At that, Davis stilled, his gaze flicking back and forth between her and Rex. The energy in the air was electric, but not in a good way. Not like what Margery felt with Rex. Suddenly it hit her what was going on. Rex might not be a shifter, but he was still a dominant male. Which meant these two might act like morons in their need to prove who was stronger. Her animal understood why her packmates were like that, but it still drove her crazy when the males, and occasionally females, went at each other's throats for no good reason. As one of the nurturers in the pack, she often had to defuse tricky situations.

Stepping closer to Rex she slid her arm through his, hoping that by showing Davis she accepted Rex as a friend and packmate it would tone down whatever was going on with him. "Rex has been a big help tonight, Davis."

"I'll bet," he muttered, his dark gaze going icy as he raked it over Rex.

Next to her Rex tensed, but he didn't say a word. Luckily Sarah chose that moment to come bounding through the swinging door. "I was out back taking out the trash and just saw a party bus pull up. I think we're about to get slammed again."

Relief slid through Margery. They were stocked for now, but that didn't mean she couldn't head to the back and whip up a few things to keep herself busy. Especially if Rex decided to stay. She still wasn't sure what his intentions were. Well, other than wanting to sleep with her. Withdrawing her arm, she turned to Rex who watched her intently. "Thank you for your help tonight but you don't need to stay with Davis here. We should be fine."

"I'm staying." There was no give to his voice or his expression.

Was that relief she felt that he was staying? When the door jingled again and a group of giggling, drunk college-aged kids stumbled in, she decided not to argue. "I'll be in the back if you need me."

"I'll join you," Davis said as he rounded the counter, heading straight through the swinging door before she could respond.

Rex looked like he wanted to say something, but just gritted his teeth and turned back to one of the registers.

Sighing, Margery headed to the back, unsure if she was disappointed or glad that Davis had interrupted what was sure to have been a scorching kiss. She knew Rex would have to leave before sunrise, but she wondered if he'd attempt to kiss her again before he left.

She definitely wouldn't stop him.

CHAPTER FOUR

"It was sweet of you to come, but I think I'm good for now," she said to Davis as she slid another tray of finished cupcakes into the waiting area. She'd made extra of her two most popular cupcakes—red velvet with cream cheese icing and chocolate with chocolate buttercream icing—and they were practically all gone. Thank God for starving college kids.

When she turned back around she found Davis barely a foot away. He had a little flour on his apron but he'd been incredibly neat and efficient. "I'd like to stay," he said quietly, his dark eyes glittering with something she recognized.

But really wished she didn't. On instinct she took a step back and knocked into the tray holder. "That's okay." Crap, she so didn't need a packmate coming on to her. Especially not now when she was feeling so out of sorts and ridiculously horny. Maybe he scented what she was feeling for Rex.

Davis shoved his hands in the front two pockets of his apron, but kept his gaze on her. "Are you seeing anyone?"

Even though she normally preferred bluntness, she inwardly cringed, not wanting to do this now. Davis was very good looking, but he wasn't her mate. If he was, she'd have figured it out a long time ago since they'd been packmates for years. Unlike most of her female packmates, she didn't mess around with any males in the pack. Probably because she'd seen what having a true mate could be like and she wanted that for herself. While she'd had short-term relationships, she usually ended things when it was clear there was no mating pull. "No, but I'm not interested in anyone."

Davis tilted his head toward the front of the store. "What about the vampire?"

"I'm not with him either. I'm just not..." She wasn't sure how to put it into words so she didn't finish her thought.

He let out a sigh, his expression relaxing. "I've been holding off making a move for a while, but lately you've seemed more open to, you know."

A smile tugged at her lips when she realized this wasn't about intense feelings he'd been harboring. It was clear he was just looking for something casual.

"Yeah, I do know." Because she'd been feeling restless and turned on, she'd likely been putting off a certain vibe to some of the males in the pack. Not intentionally but when her wolf got restless, others would know whether she wanted them to or not. "Are things going to be weird between us now?"

Half-smiling, he shook his head and closed the distance between them. He pulled her into a hug. "Can't blame a wolf for trying," he murmured, his breath warm against the top of her head.

As she started to step out of his embrace, she nearly fell back as Rex body-slammed him. Davis flew through the air, landing against one of the freezer doors with a thud.

Oh, shit.

His claws and canines immediately came out as he and Rex simultaneously rushed each other. They growled and snarled as they started pummeling each other with their fists, claws and teeth. In seconds they were rolling on the ground like maniacal cubs, not trained and disciplined supernatural males.

Margery knew better than to get in the middle of a fight with two dominant males but she wasn't going to let them ruin her kitchen. Grabbing a huge bowl of melted butter, she used her shifter agility and jumped onto the nearest flat prep station. She tossed the warm butter down on their heads and to her surprise they both shouted in disbelief and rolled back.

As the mess trailed down Rex's hair and into his face, she cursed herself for imagining what it would be like to lick it off him. The thought of eating just butter was weird, but not the thought of tracing her tongue over every single inch of him.

"What the hell is going on in here?" Sarah demanded from the doorway, staring at all of them as if they'd lost their minds.

Margery didn't wait for them to answer. She ripped off her apron and tossed it at Davis. "You two clean this crap up. And find a way to work with each other the rest of the night because I'm leaving."

"Margery," Rex said as he stood, more of the butter dripping down onto his shoulders. Why did he have to look so adorable? "Please let me apologize—"

"No." She shook her head, not wanting to hear it. The thing was, she wasn't even angry. She knew exactly why Rex was acting all crazy and territorial. When Sarah had told Margery that she'd make a move on Rex if Margery didn't, the strangest possessive urge had welled up inside her, making her wolf claw at her in a way she never did. So she understood the vampire's primal urges.

Which was exactly why she couldn't be around him any longer. Distance was the only thing that could help. She hoped. Then she'd have to talk to Grant about rescinding his offer to Rex. They couldn't have a vampire in their pack. Not when he was making Margery want to climb the walls with an undeniable need she wouldn't give into.

No, no, no. She refused to believe what her wolf was telling her. Refused to even think the words, much less admit the truth aloud. He wasn't her destined mate. "Sarah, you're in charge. Call me if there's a problem." She didn't wait for a response as she hurried to the front of the shop.

Her keys were in her pants pocket and she didn't need her purse. Sarah could just bring it to her later. It was a little after midnight and the second she stepped outside the crisp April air rolled over her. Not quite summer but a little warmer than their normal spring. The parking lot was nearly deserted except for pack vehicles and Rex's SUV. Inhaling deeply she savored the fresh scent of the ocean nearby. It calmed her—sort of.

Nothing could actually do that right now. Nothing but the mysterious and sexy vampire back in her bakery. As she slid her key into the ignition her door was wrenched open. She turned, ready to tell Rex to back off when a female she didn't recognize slammed something into Margery's neck. She hadn't even scented the female. Her adrenaline was pumping so hard that her senses were all jumbled up.

Cold agony slid through her veins, nearly immobilizing her. But she refused to go down without a fight. Punching out, she slammed her fist into the female's nose, the hit almost as weak as a human.

The female laughed as she took the punch, the sound grating against Margery's senses. Her vision blurred as another shot of pain battered against all her nerve endings. What the hell...

Silver.

The bitch had shot her up with silver. Calling on her only remaining strength, Margery let her wolf take over, knowing her animal side would protect her as best as she could. The woman cursed as she shifted, the last sound Margery heard before she succumbed to blackness.

* * *

"I'm going to smell like butter all night," Davis muttered as he watched Margery go.

Rex kept his gaze pinned on the wolf, resisting the urge to go after Margery. He refused to make her feel cornered when it was clear she needed space.

Davis finally glanced back at him and held up his hands in mock surrender—though his body was tense and it was clear he was ready for another attack. Rex had lost complete control before, tackling the other male like a new vampire not in control of his baser needs. It was embarrassing, especially since he'd done it in front of the female he wanted more than he'd ever wanted any other.

"Feel free to let the pack know Margery's off limits," he finally managed to grit out.

Davis watched him warily. "You must have heard our conversation. You knew she wasn't interested in me. Why'd you attack?"

Rex had heard it and it'd pissed him off beyond reason. He didn't owe the wolf an explanation but if he was going to assimilate into a wolf pack he knew he needed to be somewhat diplomatic. "You offered her something *casual*. Margery deserves more than that." If she ever allowed Rex to touch her there would be nothing remotely casual about it. "That was your first strike. Then you touched what's mine." The guttural words were out before he could stop himself. Even the image of Davis's arms wrapped around Margery's lithe form made him crazy. That primal thing built up inside him, pushing at all his rationalization, stripping him back to who he'd been when he'd just turned into a vampire.

And it scared the shit out of him.

Davis's dark eyes flared pure wolf for a moment, likely from Rex's threatening tone, but then his entire body relaxed. "Damn, vampire. Get that shit out of your hair then go after her."

"Yeah, me and bozo here have this covered. Go see Margery. She deserves some happiness," Sarah said, still lingering in the doorway.

"Bozo?" Davis asked mildly.

"Yeah. That's what you are for poaching on another male's territory. What the hell's the matter with you?"

"It's not like I knew..."

Rex tuned out their conversation as he stuck his head under the faucet of one of the industrial sized stainless steel sinks. After washing out what he could using the antibacterial soap he wiped the last remnants of butter from his face and neck. He didn't give a shit about his clothes, he just wanted to find Margery and explain—and apologize for—his asinine behavior.

When he exited the kitchen, Davis was still cleaning up under another sink behind him. In the main store there were half a dozen people in line, some quietly murmuring to each other as Sarah rang them up. After a quick nod at her, he hurried out into the parking lot and immediately stilled as he rounded the side of the building.

Margery's Jeep was there.

Heart beating an erratic tattoo, he raced to the driver's door and realized it wasn't quite closed, as if someone had shut it but not pushed hard enough. He pulled the door open and full-fledged fear erupted inside him, clawing away at his insides.

Her key was still in the ignition and remnants of Margery's shredded clothes lined the front seat. There was no way in hell she'd have shifted in the middle of the parking lot unless she'd been under threat.

The thought of anything threatening her made him see red.

Forcing himself to remain calm, he looked around, focusing on any potential threats. Whatever had happened to Margery, he was going to find her. Because he refused to believe otherwise. As he scanned the perimeter of the parking lot he inhaled deeply, taking in all the scents. In a place this busy, it was damn near impossible to sift through everything. He'd learned long ago to consciously ignore the majority of scents and sounds around him except when he needed to home in on something.

Somehow he locked down his fear for Margery, keeping it at bay as he took control of his senses. Along the main road there was a couple strolling down the sidewalk, hand-in-hand. On his other side he spotted a couple making out in the front seat of a car. Dismissing any threats, he leaned into the front seat and inspected everything.

The sharp scent of fear and anger permeated the air. Margery was afraid but she was also pissed. A heavy dose of guilt slammed into him. If he hadn't been fighting with Davis like an out of control male she'd have never come out here by herself. He picked up part of the shirt she'd been wearing. He already had her scent but he inhaled, pulling it deeper into his memory. As he did, something slick and almost shiny caught his eye. Leaning down toward the seat he zeroed in on the substance. Before he gently touched it, he knew what it was.

Colloidal silver. His finger burned as he swiped against it, but he ignored the discomfort. Right now finding Margery was all that mattered. The terror splintering through him would have to take a back seat. He had to keep a level head if he wanted to save her.

She wouldn't carry silver around with her. Someone must have injected her with it. It was the only thing that made sense of the mess left behind. There weren't too many reasons for her to have gone wolf in a semi-public place. But if she was being threatened or attacked to the point her inner animal felt the need to take over, her human side wouldn't have had a choice. Silver in her bloodstream would be excruciating but it wouldn't kill her. Not at her age. That knowledge was the only thing that kept his primal side at bay. Barely.

He pulled out his phone, ready to call Grant when his phone buzzed with an incoming text.

If you want to see that pretty shifter again get in your SUV and drive west. Wait for instructions. Tell anyone in that wolf pack and the bitch dies.

Icy tendrils wrapped around his throat, squeezing tight. Someone had to be watching him. After the text followed a picture of a brown and white wolf with a shackle around one of its legs. It was connected to a thick chain. Rex almost crushed his phone in his hand. He'd never seen Margery shift but he had no doubt that was her. She lay there, her head on her paw with her eyes closed. He prayed she was just unconscious.

Without knowing what her kidnapper wanted he couldn't let Grant know about this. Not yet. He was going to get her back.

Rex strode toward the front of the parking lot where he'd parked, his movements jerky. Margery had left her Jeep at the side of the building, somewhat out of sight, but there hadn't been many spots when he'd arrived.

As Rex reached his SUV, Davis strode out the front door. Rex could see Sarah inside at the cash register helping the last customer while the others were now sitting at the high-top tables eating their pastries.

"Hey, Rex," Davis called out, but Rex ignored him.

Jumping into the front seat of his SUV, he threw it into reverse before hauling ass out of there. He didn't know if he was being watched and he couldn't be seen talking to anyone. As he pulled onto the main road, his phone rang.

Hell, maybe he was being watched. It was from the same number as the text. He answered immediately. "Yeah."

"I'm going to give you an address and you're going to plug it into your GPS system and follow the directions exactly," a female said.

"Who is this?"

"The female who has your bitch. Saw you two cozying up at her bakery. Can't believe you're hooking up with a shifter but I guess there's no accounting for taste with a piece of garbage who hunts his own kind." Her voice dripped with unconcealed disgust.

Rex's grip tightened on the steering wheel, those icy fingers around his throat squeezing even more. So this had to do with his job. Shit. This could be about pure payback. And God knew he'd made plenty of enemies. "What do you want from me?"

She quickly rattled off an address then said, "Go there. You'll be met by a vampire. You're going to take him to Stanley then we're going to do an even trade for your shifter."

Like hell. "That's not how trades work," he snarled. "I'll meet you at a centralized place and we'll do an even trade out in the open." Unfortunately he didn't have Stanley. The only good thing was, this female had no clue the vamp was dead.

"No. I'm in charge and these are the parameters of my deal. As soon as we're done here, throw your phone out the window. If you don't, I'll know. Be there in ten minutes or she dies. Bring backup and she dies." The female hung up.

Rex let out a savage curse, but did as she said and threw his phone out the window. He input the address while driving, his hand actually shaking. He was over two hundred years old and his fucking hand shook. If this unknown female hurt Margery…he couldn't even think about that. No, he had to stay focused on his mission. Then he'd destroy whoever had taken her.

Once the address registered he realized it wasn't far, around ten minutes out. Maybe less. The female had given him just enough time to get there and ensure he couldn't set a trap. From the dashboard map he realized how close it was to Charmaine's bed and breakfast where he'd killed Stanley. For a brief moment he thought about contacting her and getting more intel on what Stanley had been up to and who his associates had been. But he didn't trust her enough.

He used his Onstar system to call Grant. He rarely used the system but kept it as a backup. Now more than ever he was thankful to have it.

The alpha picked up on the fourth ring, sounding distracted. "Yeah."

"It's me. Margery's been taken by an unknown female. Probable silver poisoning. There might be more than one kidnapper. I don't know for sure but I'm guessing it was vamps. This has something to do with the male I was hunting because she wants to do a trade." Which he would have done, if Stanley was still alive. "She insisted I throw out my phone so it's possible someone's watching me." At least they couldn't see into his SUV with the dark tint on the windows. He quickly repeated the address.

"I'm putting together a team as we speak," Grant said, his voice clipped and tense.

Rex could hear movement and low murmurs in the background. "It needs to be small and you guys better be fucking invisible. They'll kill her if they sense backup." Under normal circumstances he'd never order an alpha around but he didn't care now.

"We will be. Take care of yourself. We're going to get her back." The deadly edge to his voice left no doubt that Grant would follow through. Margery was his packmate and if she'd been around since Grant's father was alpha, there was no way in hell he'd let this go unpunished. Whoever had taken her would die.

And Rex wanted to be the one who meted out that sentence.

As he neared what should be the last turnoff according to the map, he slowed. The road was about a mile before the one leading to Charmaine's, but the landscape was basically the same. Farmland and pecan trees. He didn't like how open it was but the night and trees should give him enough cover if necessary. As the road turned into a dead end, his GPS announced that he'd arrived at his destination.

He turned it off, then slid into the backseat. Crouching low he surveyed his surroundings as he pulled out a few explosive devices he always kept with him. Without knowing how many threats were out there he was going to be as prepared as possible. There was a dilapidated picket fence around a big spread of land that had pecan trees surrounding it. Behind it he could barely make out a barn-like structure through a thicket of trees. Withdrawing one of his blades, he slowly opened one of the doors and stepped out.

A soft whistling sound was his only warning. As he dove to the ground, an arrow skimmed his upper arm, ripping his shirt open, but didn't penetrate skin. Pumped up on adrenaline he barely felt the burning sensation over his bare arm. But someone had shot at him with a silver-tipped arrow.

He might be used to tracking down vamps and bringing them back alive, but this time he was ending whoever was behind this swiftly and with brutal force.

CHAPTER FIVE

Margery shifted against the dusty concrete floor, cursing her chain. She tried to focus on her surroundings but a dull throb of pain threaded through every fiber of her being. Being in wolf form helped, but the agony of the silver in her bloodstream was making her weak and disoriented.

Though the room she was being held captive in was dark, she could still see enough thanks to her extrasensory abilities. A wooden ladder was propped up against a trapdoor in the ceiling. She could scent normal foliage, moldy hay and pecan trees. She could even scent traces of the ocean, but the salty tinge in the air was incredibly faint. Which gave her hope that they hadn't gone too far. Maybe ten or so miles from the main beach strip. Margery couldn't know for sure but she didn't think they would have been able to go far because the woman who'd taken her was a vampire. Not with sunrise only a couple hours away. Her sense of time was skewed along with everything else but her animal sensed that not much time had elapsed. Her animal had also sensed the female was a vamp right before she'd fallen unconscious.

When the trapdoor opened, Margery laid her muzzle on her paws, feigning sleep as she kept her breathing and heartbeat as steady as possible.

"She's still out," the female murmured.

"We should just kill her now," a male said.

Margery forced herself not to tense or change her breathing, but if these two tried to kill her, she was taking one of them with her. She might be weak right now but if one of them got close enough, she'd rip their throat out.

"Not yet," the female snapped as she shut the door. "She's our only bargaining chip for Stanley..." Her voice grew fainter as she left, but Margery couldn't even hear them walking away.

She also hadn't heard them approach. Either she was weaker than she thought or they'd used their vampiric gift of speed to sneak up on the door—or they hadn't left at all. Maybe they were just waiting to see if she'd been faking being asleep.

Margery remained unmoving for long minutes and when no other sounds came, she took a risk and stood up on shaky legs. When the trapdoor didn't fly open, she tugged on the chain with her paw. It scraped against the ground noisily.

Automatically she tensed, but the door remained shut.

The silver kept burning her insides in a way that was nearly indescribable other than pure pain, but she was becoming more lucid, stronger. Her legs and paws were thicker than when in human form so she knew her only chance of escape was to shift forms.

Taking a deep breath, she fought through the pain of the poison in her system and forced herself to undergo the change. A different kind of pain, more discomfort than anything, rippled through her as skin replaced fur and her bones shifted and realigned.

In moments she was human again, crouching on the dusty ground on all fours. But she smiled when the shackle slid off her slim wrist. Hell yeah.

Now all she had to do was get out of this prison. As she stood, she felt more of her strength returning thanks to the change back from wolf to human. And the pain from the silver was more of a dull throb affecting her muscles now. Still incredibly uncomfortable, but she could deal with that. Discomfort was better than death.

At over two hundred years old she was strong. Clearly more so than those vampires had realized. They had to be young.

On bare feet she started climbing the wooden rungs, careful on each step. She might be regaining her strength but she was unsteady. Still no sounds from above. As she reached the trapdoor, she tentatively pressed her palm against it.

It pushed up half an inch then stopped. A chain rattled against the door. With the slight opening she could see the end of it bolted to a concrete slab. Taking a deep breath, she called on all her strength and shoved up against the door.

She felt the force of the impact all the way to her bones. The door snapped up, pulling the chain free from the ground as it flipped open. Because of the awkward angle she lost her balance and started to fall. Scrambling, she tried to grab the ladder but her reflexes were too sluggish after that use of her waning strength.

She bit back a cry of pain as she slammed back to the ground. No sound from above. No once coming after her.

Shoving up, she started climbing the ladder again. Nothing was keeping her from getting out of here.

* * *

Rex rolled under the SUV, using his vehicle as cover from his attacker—or attackers. From this angle someone would have to get up close and personal if they wanted to shoot at him again. He almost hoped they did.

Amped up on adrenaline with the need to save Margery, he welcomed anyone trying to attack.

He ignored the sharp ping near the front left tire as he pulled out a small block of C-4. He didn't want to destroy his own SUV but he needed the diversion. Hell, he'd incinerate everything he had to get Margery back safe.

C-4 was his favorite explosive. It was stable and malleable. A perfect combination. Laying on his back, he set it on his chest and worked fast, thankful for his supernatural speed as he rigged the explosive to the underside of the gas tank in seconds. With quick fingers he slid two blasting caps into it before rolling out the other side of the SUV.

On a burst of speed, he sprinted away from the rambling house and into the pecan orchard. As he cleared the first tree, he pressed the pre-set code into his burner phone, setting the explosion off.

He'd moved deep into the orchard by the time the fiery ball of smoke and flames licked into the sky. Well out of the blast zone, he couldn't even feel the heat as he slowed in between two big trees. Using the darkness and orchard as cover, he crouched low, inhaling deeply.

Shifters.

He scented at least a dozen wolf shifters in the vicinity. And if he could, that meant the other vamp, or vamps, could too. Panic surged through him. If they smelled backup, Margery could be hurt or worse. He had to get to her.

Not caring if he was running into a trap, he scanned the area once more before drawing on all his strength and sprinting back through the orchard toward the house. As he neared the fence the wind changed and that subtle lavender scent of Margery rolled over him.

It didn't matter how faint, he knew it was her and just inhaling it was like a punch to his senses, amplifying his protective instincts. Changing directions, he bypassed the house and raced for the barn. Even though he moved at such high speeds that humans couldn't track him with the naked eye, a vamp would be able to pinpoint him and possibly attack.

Forcing himself to act like the hunter he was, he started to slow as he neared the outside of the barn—until he heard Margery scream.

His fangs and claws sprung free as he covered the remaining twenty yards to the barn. Margery screamed again and he vaguely registered it was one of anger, not fear. Following her scent and the scuffling sounds, he slammed through a wooden half-door for what might have been a stable or storage area. He didn't care what it was as he ripped the door off its hinges. Wood splintered under the force.

When he saw a trapdoor-type opening in the corner of the stable he withdrew his blade and dove through it. Maybe it was fucking stupid of him, but nothing could stop him from getting to Margery.

His boots landed on the concrete floor with a thud, puffs of dust and dirt flying everywhere.

He snarled at the sight of a female on top of a naked, struggling Margery, her clawed fingers around Margery's neck. The female vamp swiveled when she heard him, her eyes a bright amber and full of rage. Then she flew at him. Without pause he brought his blade up and sliced her head off in a clean sweep.

Before her head hit the ground, it and her fallen body turned to ash. Rex scanned the lower room, taking in every inch and shadow of the small storage area. Finding it empty, he hurried to Margery who was struggling to sit up. Cuts and gashes covered her beautiful body, though she was already healing with impressive speed. Even in the darkness he could see how pale she was.

Kneeling next to her, he pulled her to him. A potent relief that he'd never imagined surged through him when she lunged at him, wrapping her arms around his neck and plastering herself to his body in a suffocating hug.

He rubbed a hand up and down her back, just grateful she was okay. "Was she the only vamp?" he asked, needing to know how big the threat was against her.

"No," Margery rasped out as she pulled back. Immediately she wrapped her arms around herself, covering her breasts. "There was a male but I never saw his face. Just heard his voice."

Rex knew shifters didn't care about nudity too much, but Margery had to be feeling vulnerable now. That was unacceptable in any circumstance. He unbuttoned his shirt and handed it to her. The primal part of him reveled in the knowledge that his scent was now all over her.

"I don't know where he is though," she continued, sounding a little stronger, as she slid his shirt on.

Rex ached to reach out to her and help, but wasn't sure if she'd welcome it or if she'd want to gain back some control. When her fingers shook as she tried to button the shirt, he took over.

"Thank you." Her voice trembled in a way that made him want to kill that female vamp all over again.

"Your packmates are getting closer," he said instead of responding to her gratitude. She never had to thank him for saving her.

Now that he was back in control and coming down from his adrenaline high he sensed they were relatively safe. Grant and a few others were entering the barn. Their scent was strong and he heard the faint pad of paws on the ground.

"I don't want to see anyone right now," she whispered. "Make them go away."

Rex was stunned by her words. Shifters always went to their pack for comfort. It was part of what made his kind and hers so different. But he could see the pain in her eyes and would do any damn thing she wanted. Nodding, he picked up his blade and went to the ladder.

"Grant, I'm coming up." As he rose through the opening he found a naked Grant standing in the busted out entryway.

"Margery—"

"Is alive. I killed a female vamp attacking her. Did the pack find anyone else on the property?"

The alpha nodded, his expression dark. "Male vamp escaped by vehicle. Asher's tailing him now."

Rex glanced down at Margery who was still huddled on the floor and the strongest need to protect her overwhelmed him. He looked back at Grant, all his instincts demanding that he go to her, hold her, claim her in front of these shifters. "She doesn't want to see anyone and I need to get her out of here. Now." The sun would be rising soon enough and she needed to be somewhere she felt safe.

Grant frowned, likely because Margery didn't want to see anyone. For a moment it appeared as if he'd push the issue, but he just nodded. Turning his head, he barked out a few orders then focused on Rex. "Max is by the vehicles. Take one and get her back to the compound. He's going to shadow you two so you have backup—that's not up for discussion. The rest of us are going to stay and canvas the area until I'm certain there aren't any more vamps around. I'll be by Margery's place as soon as we're done." He paused again, looking down at the trapdoor, but didn't say anything else before leaving.

Rex heard him shift to his wolf form before he'd exited the barn. When Rex looked back down Margery had moved to the bottom of the stairs. She looked impossibly tired and vulnerable, her eyes even bigger in her pale face.

"Thank you and...I'm sorry for putting that on you. I'm so weak and I just..." She trailed off and he let out a savage curse.

Jumping back down, he scooped her up in his arms before she could protest. To his surprise she wrapped an arm around his neck and curled into him. He hated the circumstance, but he loved the feel of her against him. She was soft and warm, and her scent clung to him, heightening his need to protect her.

"Did they do anything other than the silver?" he asked, unsure how else to phrase it and not wanting to upset her even more.

She shook her head, her eyes growing heavy-lidded with fatigue. "No, except for the female attacking me right before you arrived. You don't have to come with me, you know. I'll be okay." She slumped against him, seeming more tired with each word. The way she curled into him so trustingly made his heart squeeze.

He snorted at her last statement. "I'm going and it's not up for discussion." Even though Rex had more questions, now wasn't the time. All he was concerned with was getting her to safety. Tightening his grip around her, he ascended the ladder and pulled her closer to him. He planned to take care of her as long as she'd let him. Hell, he'd use his inability to walk in the daylight as an excuse to stay with her today, to watch over her. No one was ever going to hurt her again. Not as long as he was alive.

CHAPTER SIX

Margery let the near-scorching water from her showerhead pound her shoulders and back as she stood under the steady fall of water. The pain from the silver poisoning had almost diminished. She was exhausted and a little jittery but she finally felt safe in her own home. Especially since Rex had come back with her. The sexy male's presence was incredibly reassuring.

Though she didn't want to get out, she'd been in here too long and couldn't keep avoiding the very concerned vampire waiting in her living room. On the drive back to the compound he'd kept her tight in his lap and she hadn't been inclined to move because his warmth and strength wrapped around her had been exactly what she'd needed. Especially with that unknown male vampire still on the loose.

Rex was proving to be sweeter than she'd thought. Not to mention he was incredibly protective. Something that had never been a huge turn on for her before. But she liked the way he'd taken charge after finding her. He'd done exactly what she'd asked by telling Grant she didn't want to see anyone. And he hadn't asked a ton of questions or tried to tell her that she needed her pack for support right now. A shifter male would have done just that. But Rex let her take back the control she'd lost without being pushy.

He was just so damn kind and concerned. Which should set off her alarm bells. She knew the vampire wanted to get her into bed. But she wanted him naked too and she knew he would never hurt her. She knew it was time to stop hiding behind her past, especially since the pull she felt toward him was the mating pull. She couldn't deny it any longer, even if she'd wanted to. So far Rex had been nothing but honest and honorable. It was just so damn hard to let go of something she'd been using as a crutch for so many years.

Sighing at herself, she shut off the shower and got out. After drying her hair until it was damp, she changed into short black and pink pajama bottoms with dogs on them and a pink tank top. Talia had gotten her the pajamas as a Christmas present, thinking the dogs were funny.

When Margery stepped out into the hall, she jerked to a halt to find Rex leaning against the wall just as she'd left him earlier. He was still rumpled and dirty and she could smell faint traces of butter. "Didn't you want to take a shower?" she asked.

He shook his head, that hazel gaze raking over the length of her body and making her nipples bead. "I wanted to make sure you were okay and...didn't want to leave you unguarded."

His words stunned her speechless for a long moment but she finally found her voice as she crossed her arms over her breasts. "Have you been waiting out here the whole time?"

He nodded, his expression unreadable.

It bothered her that she couldn't tell what he was thinking. "I'm sorry. You can—"

"Margery, I need to tell you something. You were taken because of me. I was hunting a vampire and accidentally killed him. Well, he killed himself, but that's not important. You were targeted because someone saw us together at your bakery and assumed we were together. If I'd thought it was a possibility to bring danger to you I never would have pursued you. I'm sorry." His handsome face was so stressed, so filled with guilt she couldn't help but step closer and grab his hands in hers.

"Rex, I know. The female said something about it before she tried to kill me. She was in a rage and most of her words were incomprehensible but I gathered she wanted to use me as a bargaining chip. But she planned to kill both of us—until you arrived with backup. I don't think she was very old for a vamp or very smart. She couldn't have been to take me when I'm part of a powerful pack. But, I know and I'm not angry. You really thought I would be?" There was no way she could be angry at this male. Definitely not after he'd saved her, but mainly because of who he was showing himself to be.

He nodded stiffly, watching her warily as if he didn't quite believe her.

"Well, I'm not. Why don't you shower and we can watch a movie?" She was exhausted but didn't want to go to bed just yet and didn't want to be alone. And if she was being honest with herself, she wanted him to hold her, needed to feel his touch. "I mean, if you're going to stay." She really hoped he did. The sun had already risen but maybe he didn't want to stay in her condo. Using the interior hallways and elevators he could move somewhere else if he wanted. She couldn't expect him to just drop everything for her.

Finally the tenseness in his shoulders fled. "I'm staying and if you'll allow me, I would like to offer you my blood."

Blinking, her eyes widened at his offer. Vampire blood had supernatural healing power and would help her kick the lingering sluggishness from the poison. Otherwise time was the only thing that would work. But vampires *never* offered their blood to anyone. Not that she knew of. It was a mate thing. The implication of that stole her breath for a moment. "Rex, that's..." She didn't know what to say. It would be too weird to accept it, but part of her really wanted to. The thought of drinking blood should freak her out, but everything about Rex called to her. Part of her wanted to find out what he tasted like.

An abrupt knock at her front door made her jump like a cub. Inwardly she cursed her reaction.

"It's Grant. He texted while you were in the shower," Rex said then turned away before she could respond.

She immediately felt the loss of touching him as he withdrew his hands and made his way to her front door. She fell in step behind him, her bare feet silent against the hardwood floors. Moments later her alpha stood in the foyer of her place.

Without a word Grant pulled her into a tight hug. Being held by her alpha soothed her wolf in a way almost no one else could. Except...she'd actually felt safer being held by Rex. Later she'd examine that, but for now she returned Grant's hug, knowing he needed to be reassured his packmate was safe.

"I'm so sorry this happened, Margery." Grant's voice was rough, uneven and so out of character.

She squeezed him tight then stepped back. "I'm okay. I promise. They didn't do anything other than poison me and then that maniac tried to kill me." Which were both terrible things, but she knew Grant had been worried about sexual assault just as Rex had been earlier. "Did you find out who the male was?" She'd heard someone with the female vampire and she'd heard Rex and Grant's conversation earlier about the male who escaped them.

Jaw tight, Grant shook his head. "Davis lost the guy, but we will find him. If there's an unknown in my territory he'll only be able to hide for so long."

"I've got a file on Stanley, but clearly it's not detailed enough. I'll reach out to my client about Stanley's former associates and we can start digging into who could have possibly wanted to help him." Rex's voice was as grim as his expression.

Margery could see the rage simmering just beneath his surface. On instinct she reached out for him, wrapping her arm around his trim waist. Her inner wolf sighed in contentment the moment they made contact. Pleasure surged through her when he didn't pause, just slid his solid arm around her shoulders and pulled her close.

Grant didn't seem surprised at their affection as he nodded at both of them. "Let me know as soon as he gets back to you. For now, you two get some damn sleep. We've increased the security and no one is getting in here. I'm staying close to the compound today so let me know if you need me. And, before you ask, I've already told the pack to give you some space until you're ready. I'm pretty sure they'll only give you today alone," he said wryly.

That, she believed. But a day was enough to rest and decompress from what had happened. She wanted to ask him about her bakery but at this point didn't really care if he closed it for a couple days or sent some packmates to work there. "Thank you." After giving her another hug, Grant left and she was once again alone with Rex.

After his offer of blood she was feeling more off-balance than ever.

"I am going to shower," Rex said abruptly before turning and leaving her standing by the front door.

O-kay. What had that been about? Too mentally exhausted to think about it, she headed for her kitchen in search of food. Food and rest were the two cure-alls for everyone. Right now her wolf was restless though, wanting Rex's presence more than anything.

* * *

Rex tried to will his cock to go down as he pulled on a pair of jeans Margery must have left for him when he was in the shower. They smelled like Grant so he guessed the alpha must have brought them over. Rex was just glad they didn't smell like some random male. She'd left a T-shirt too but he decided to go shirtless. He wanted her as aware of him as possible.

Something had shifted between them since they'd returned to her place. She hadn't minded his touch, had even reached for him. He wasn't sure if there was more to it than just her needing simple comfort. Either way, he liked it. He found her in the living room curled up on the couch with a book in hand. All the floor to ceiling length drapes were closed, so the room was incredibly dim. He wouldn't know it was daylight if his internal clock didn't tell him. She must have pulled the hurricane shutters in place, which he found incredibly thoughtful.

Putting her book down, she smiled when she saw him. The open way she greeted him stroked against his senses in the most erotic way. Almost immediately her smile disappeared as her gaze raked hungrily over his bare chest. Her mouth parted slightly, her full lips so damn kissable he had to restrain himself from groaning out loud.

If she kept looking at him like that he didn't think he'd be able to show any restraint. Not if she gave him the green light. If that happened...his body tightened in anticipation. Just imagining her underneath him, completely surrendering to the electric heat between them, made it hard to think straight.

"Your eyes are doing that glowing thing again," she said, drawing his gaze away from her very kissable lips to her eyes.

"Seems to be a permanent thing around you." The words escaped before he could stop himself.

"Can you control it?" There was only curiosity in her voice, nothing to indicate it bothered her.

"For the most part." He just didn't want to. No, Rex wanted Margery to see all of him. He was a vampire and he wasn't going to hide that part of himself. "Did you..." He wanted to ask her if she'd given any thought to his offer of blood, but couldn't force the question out. She'd seemed so shocked by his offer before and he didn't want to hear her rejection, but the thought of sharing his blood with her made him so hard it hurt. Clearing his throat, he continued. "Did you still want to watch a movie?"

She nodded and reached for one of the remote controls on her wooden coffee table. "I wasn't sure if you'd be too tired. Honestly, don't feel like you need to babysit me."

He snorted as he joined her on the couch, sitting closer than she'd apparently expected if her soft exhale was any indication. "I only sleep a few hours during the day." At his age it was all he needed unless he'd been seriously injured and had to heal.

"If you're sure..." She trailed off as she started pressing buttons on one of the remote controls. Moments later a list of movies came up on the screen. "These are all in my queue. Some I've seen, others I've been waiting to watch."

He laughed out loud as he scanned the selection. "They're all vampire, werewolf or zombie movies."

She grinned, taking his breath away. "I know. I watch the vamp and werewolf movies mainly because I think they're more comedy than horror but I love zombie movies. And there's a new television show about zombies I'm not caught up with this season. Totally my not-so-guilty pleasure."

It struck him as funny that she enjoyed zombies. "You pick then."

She didn't argue, just chose the current season of the television show and settled back against the couch. The scent of her desire lingered in the air, subtle but strong enough that he had no doubt she wanted him. After what she'd been through though, he wanted to tread lightly.

"You might have to fill me in a little," he said, scooting a couple inches closer after about ten minutes had passed. To his surprise, she subtly shifted closer, leaning toward him. But he didn't want subtle. Taking a chance, he wrapped his arm around her shoulders.

In response she closed the last few inches between them and laid her head half on his shoulder, half on his chest as he pulled her close. She wrapped an arm around his waist and curled her body into his. The feel of her fingers gliding across his bare skin made him shudder.

Something warm and peaceful settled in his chest, the rightness of it taking him off guard. For the first time in his life he felt almost calm inside. Being in Margery's presence had made something primal inside him flare to life, but this was different.

"His wife died," she murmured, referring to the current male on the screen. Every few minutes she'd tell him things about the characters until eventually she stopped talking, her head and body completely going lax against him. He didn't give a damn about the show, only that she was lying in his arms, relaxed and trusting. That surge of protectiveness rose up again, so strong he had to let out a deep breath to release the pressure building in his chest.

Considering what she'd been through at the hands of vampires—twice now—it said a lot for how much she trusted him to fall asleep in his arms. He knew enough about shifters that her wolf wouldn't let her guard down unless she felt safe. The knowledge pleased him more than he imagined possible. It also helped solidify his intent to pursue her hard. If her wolf trusted him, he'd already overcome the biggest hurdle because he had no doubt the most female part of her wanted him. He planned to use that to his full advantage.

Pulling her tighter to him, he turned off the television and closed his eyes. Very soon he was going to have her underneath him, begging for more and shouting his name. He hadn't thought he was tired, but sleep came fast, taking him under with dreams of a beautiful shifter with big eyes and full, kissable lips.

CHAPTER SEVEN

M argery inhaled Rex's masculine scent before she forced her eyes open. She wasn't sure how long they'd been on the couch cuddled together but she guessed it must have been a few hours. She didn't want to move, but she didn't think she'd be able to go back to sleep draped across him. The only way she'd do that was if she put some distance between them. Otherwise she was far too tempted to start kissing and licking across his delectable chest. As she started to push up, his arm tightened around her, pulling her closer.

His eyes opened halfway, heavy-lidded with undeniable hunger as he watched her. "Where are you going?" he murmured, his sexy voice thick with sleep.

She started to tell him she was headed to bed but realized she didn't want to go. At least not alone. It had been a long time since she'd been with anyone, but Rex had proved himself to be an honorable male, and he also made her hotter than any male ever had. Considering how at ease her wolf was with him, she decided to make herself completely vulnerable.

Moving quickly, she clutched his shoulder before she slid a leg over his waist and straddled him. He was already rock hard in his jeans, his erection pushing insistently at the juncture between her thighs.

He woke up completely, the lingering sleep fleeing in an instant. The soft glow to his eyes was intense. He watched her carefully as he slid his hands up her thighs. The feel of his hands skating over her bare legs made her shiver. She wanted to feel those long, callused fingers stroking everywhere, wanted to get lost in the pleasure she knew they could find with each other.

His hands stopped on her hips, flexing around her as if he thought she might try to leave. That definitely wasn't happening. When he still didn't say anything, just watched her, she figured she might have to make the first move. Something made her hesitate.

She'd told him that she didn't want anything to do with vampires and even though things were different between them now, she wanted to put him at ease. And she really wanted to feel his mouth on her. It didn't matter that they hadn't known each other that long, her heart and body knew all they needed to about this male. And their joining was an eventual thing. She felt it bone deep and didn't see the point in putting off the pleasure when she could take it now. More than anything she wanted her scent all over him, wanted every female to know that this male belonged to her. The possessiveness she experienced rattled her.

Before she could change her mind she tugged on the hem of her tank top and pulled it over her head. This was the clearest message she could send him.

The rush of air combined with the heated look he ran over her bare breasts, as if he'd physically caressed them, made her nipples tighten into hard points.

"I should ask if you're sure about this, but...I'm a selfish bastard," he muttered before crushing his mouth to hers.

The kiss took her off guard as he slanted his head and invaded her mouth with his tongue, moving on her with pure dominance. She clutched at his broad shoulders, her fingers digging into his hard flesh as he flicked his tongue against hers. She teased him right back, loving the give and take to their kiss.

There was nothing sweet about his kisses, they were demanding and a little unsteady. As if Rex wasn't quite in control of himself. That was fine with her. She felt out of control too, the need building inside her a wonderful, unexpected and slightly scary thing.

She rubbed her bare breasts against his chest, shuddering at the feel of her nipples brushing against rock hard muscle. He was pure, ripped perfection. Seeing his naked torso was one thing, but feeling it against hers was heaven.

As she slid her hands down his muscular chest, tracing her fingers along the hard lines and striations of his powerful body, heat flooded between her thighs. Just feeling his strength made her inner walls tighten and her body light up with a need he had to scent.

When he groaned into her mouth she dug her fingers into his waist, holding tight to him. He rolled his hips against hers and before she realized what he intended, he'd flipped her onto her back, stretching out on top of her as he continued to stroke his tongue against hers. Anticipation hummed through her, an unsteady erratic lashing against her nerves.

Gently nipping her bottom lip between his teeth, he pulled back a fraction. "This doesn't have to go beyond kissing."

"I'll kill you if it doesn't," she murmured, wanting everything he had to offer.

He laughed, the rich sound reverberating through her entire body, making all her nerve endings sing in the most wonderful awareness. "I'm so glad you said that." He kissed along her jaw, cupping one of her breasts in his hand as he raked his fangs along the column of her neck.

She shuddered at the feel of his teeth, not out of fear, but a building need. She'd never thought to be turned on by a vampire like this but... "You can drink from me if you want." She could feel that the poison was gone from her system or she wouldn't have offered.

His big body jerked above hers and he drew his head back, looking down at her with bright, glowing eyes. Hers widened at the sight.

"You're certain?" His voice was a hoarse whisper.

She nodded, her nipples tightening even harder. The thought of him drinking from her was impossibly erotic. While she had no experience in that area something told her that Rex would make it very enjoyable. She squeezed her legs around his waist, rolling her hips against him. It was a little embarrassing how wet she was. She wanted her shorts and his jeans off so she could feel him hard and hot right where she needed him most.

"That turns you on." It wasn't exactly a question, that hoarseness still there, as if the truth stunned him.

It stunned her too, but she knew what she wanted. "What do you think?"

He was silent for a moment, his jaw tight as he appeared to try to find his voice. "Lift your hips," he finally demanded.

She complied immediately as he leaned back, positioned perfectly between her legs. In seconds he'd removed her shorts and panties. The look on his face once she was bared to him made her feel worshipped. As if she was the only woman that mattered. The gleam of his fangs peeking out from his lips made him even hotter.

She wanted to reach out and touch him, to run her hands over every inch of his delectable body—and she really wanted to strip his pants off—but he looked as if he was walking a knife's edge of control as he watched her.

His breathing was raspy and when he lifted one of her legs, he shuddered as he feathered kisses along her inner calf. Taking his time, he kissed and licked a path up one leg, stopping right at her upper thigh. High up, but not high enough to give her what she needed. What she craved. His warm breath teased her sensitive skin, ratcheting her need up higher.

She rolled her hips, trying to make her impatience known, but he just chuckled wickedly, knowing exactly what he was doing as he started on her other leg. Each time his fangs skimmed her skin, her inner walls clenched. And each time they did, Rex groaned as he scented her need.

"You're driving me crazy," he whispered as he reached the top of her other thigh.

She wanted to respond but couldn't get her voice to work. All she could do was tense with anticipation as she waited for him to kiss between her thighs. Thankfully he decided not to tease her any longer.

When he bent his head between her legs she slid her fingers through his short hair, clutching his head as his tongue flicked out against her clit.

The stroke was light, barely there and definitely not enough. She groaned in frustration and he let out another one of those wicked-sounding laughs. Her toes curled.

Spreading her thighs wider to give him more access, the coil of tension inside her snapped when he covered her wet pussy with his mouth. Teasing and stroking, his tongue lashed against her clit as he quickly found the rhythm she needed.

Without her having to tell him, he seemed to read her body expertly. When he slid two fingers inside her at once she jerked at the unexpected but welcome sensation. He pushed deep then withdrew them, excruciatingly slow, while his tongue continued the intense rhythm against her clit.

It was maddening and perfect at the same time. Unable to bite back her groan, she let go of any semblance of control. Her place was well insulated but it didn't matter if anyone heard her. Hell, the entire condo could for all she cared. She wanted everyone to know this male was hers. "Rex." She repeated his name as he continued pleasuring her. The more she said his name, the more worked up he seemed to get, his teasing strokes growing unsteady. "I'm close."

With a growl, he buried his fingers deep inside her and tweaked her clit with his other hand, lightly rubbing the sensitive bundle of nerves between his thumb and forefinger. She arched off the couch at the abrupt action as her climax slammed into her.

The surge of pleasure battering all her nerve endings was too much. Her abdomen tightened and all her muscles pulled taut with need as she fell straight into the most perfect orgasm she'd ever experienced.

The little waves of pleasure kept flowing through her until she fell lax against the couch, her breathing harsh and her heartbeat uneven. "That was amazing." She'd barely gotten the words out of her mouth before he'd moved with supernatural speed, covering her lips with his.

She loved the taste of her own pleasure on Rex's lips, loved that he was now covered in her scent. Every female would know this male was hers, soothing her inner wolf immensely. Reaching between them she yanked at his jeans, nearly ripping the button out as she tugged it free. He helped her shove them down and off, kicking them free of the couch.

When he sat up, revealing every inch of himself, her mouth watered. She'd guessed he was big from the erection she'd felt but the sight of him made her lips curve up as she reached for his thick length.

He might not be a shifter but the male was pure alpha so she knew he'd want to be on top, something that was more than fine with her for now.

She wanted to experience everything he had to offer and to give him as much pleasure as he'd given her.

She wrapped her fingers around his cock. "Soon this is going to be in my mouth," she promised.

He let out a savage groan at her words before she guided him to her entrance. Now more than ever she was glad supernatural beings couldn't carry diseases because she could feel him inside her with no barrier. His gaze was electric, giving her no doubt how much he wanted her as he slid deep inside her. The sensation of being filled by him stole her breath.

She held his face, pulling him down to her as he began thrusting hard. Their mouths clashed at the same pace as their bodies, harsh and primal. Each time he slammed into her, she moaned at the sensation.

It had been too long since she'd found release with someone and her body was beyond primed for another orgasm. But not just anyone would make her react this way.

As Rex tore his mouth from hers and raked his fangs against the pulse point in her throat, everything inside her turned molten.

"Drink," she demanded, fingers clenching his hair.

He didn't pause or ask if she was sure, just struck her vein sharp and fast. A shot of pure pleasure slammed through her at the sensation of his fangs sinking into her. When he started sucking, she lost complete control, her body going into a freefall as another, harder climax rippled through her.

As soon as she let go, Rex followed, drinking from her as he came, his tugs and groans against her neck making her crazy. She dug her fingers into his back, knowing she'd mark him and not caring. She wanted her mark on him, just as he was marking her with his teeth, scent and his own bruising grip.

Arching her back, her breasts rubbed against his chest, the additional friction stimulating her even more until they both collapsed against the couch.

Rex withdrew his fangs, and she immediately mourned the loss of that connection until he gently nuzzled her neck, flicking his tongue over the small wounds. With her healing capabilities and his attentions she doubted she'd have markings by the time night fell.

She gently ran her fingers up and down his back until he pulled his head up. Still half-hard inside her, his gaze was intense and so full of adoration, she couldn't help the sappy smile that spread across her face.

"Too tired for more?" he asked quietly, the pure male question making her laugh.

She shook her head and before she'd answered audibly, he moved off the couch, clutching her to him with a possessive intimacy as he made his way to her bedroom.

Oh yes, today was going to be long and wonderful. Deep down she hoped it was the start of something more. Whatever was happening between them, whether it was the mating pull or not, she'd never felt anything like it and she wanted the chance to see where this relationship could lead.

CHAPTER EIGHT

"**A**nything new?" Grant asked, seated across from Rex at his desk.

Rex scanned the newest email he'd received from Pascal, the male who'd hired him to hunt down Stanley. Rex had contacted him, making it clear he wanted every single bit of information on the dead vampire. A week had passed since Margery had been kidnapped and they were still trying to hunt down the male who'd gotten away.

It was after sunset, but Rex had been up working for hours before coming over to see the alpha at his home. Talia was at work and Margery was downstairs with a couple of her packmates eating. He shook his head. "Not really. Just more trivial background information on Daria and Franz." Daria was the female Rex had killed; they were ninety-nine percent certain Franz was the male who had escaped.

According to Pascal, the two had left the coven about a month before Stanley stole from him. Pascal hadn't connected the three of them as working together, but a couple of his coven members had confirmed the three of them had been close. It appeared that they'd wanted to start their own coven—with money stolen from Pascal.

Stupid and greedy. Unfortunately Franz didn't have any credit cards and hadn't left a paper trail anywhere. Not exactly surprising if he was on the run.

"We *will* find him." Grant's voice held a deadly promise.

Rex nodded, trying to leash his anger. He knew they would. Both he and the alpha had put out enough feelers in the supernatural community that someone would turn Franz in. But Rex wanted the male eliminated now. He needed to know the threat to Margery was completely gone. And that male was going to suffer for daring to take her. "Not soon enough."

"Margery's going back to work tomorrow," Grant said, changing the subject.

Rex gritted his teeth. This was a conversation he'd already had with the stubborn female. "I know."

A ghost of a smile touched Grant's mouth. "You want to keep her locked down twenty-four-seven." The statement was laced with mild amusement.

"Of course not...Maybe." It was his own issue and he knew he had to deal with it. She was incredibly capable and able to protect herself. He just experienced the strongest need to keep her safe from all harm. Which he knew was impossible. The female was over two hundred years old. Clearly she knew how to take care of herself and he couldn't be with her every moment of every day anyway. That knowledge didn't lessen the steady need to protect that hummed through him, a constant maddening beat. "I'm not used to feeling like this." Like he would die if anything happened to her.

Grant full-on smiled then. "Welcome to my world. Now...what's your answer?"

It had only been a week since the alpha asked him to join the pack, but Rex knew without a doubt what he wanted. "I'm in."

The alpha nodded once, not surprised. "Good. I've never seen her so happy." Continuing in a lower voice, he said, "What about living arrangements? We have more than one condo open, but..." Grant trailed off, his unspoken question clear.

"I don't know yet." Rex knew what *he* wanted; to move in with Margery permanently. After almost two hundred and fifty years of living virtually alone, the thought of sharing space with someone should scare him. Instead he embraced it like he'd never done with anything else. He wanted to wake up to Margery's face every evening and to hold her tight every time they went to sleep.

Grant's gaze narrowed a fraction, his eyes going wolf as he assessed Rex. "You don't know?"

"*I* know, I just don't know what she wants," he muttered.

He earned another smile from the alpha, taking Rex off guard again. He'd never seen Grant so relaxed. "Why haven't you asked her?"

"There's been a lot going on." He couldn't keep the defensive note out of his voice even though his answer was total bullshit. They hadn't left the bedroom much, which was fine with him.

The alpha snorted. "Or you're just too much of a pussy to tell her what you want."

Yeah, or that. What if she said no? The thought made something dark and uncomfortable settle in his chest. He didn't respond because he heard light footsteps on the stairs. A moment later Margery's subtle lavender scent invaded his senses.

Grant stood and rounded the desk. "I'll let you tell her in case you haven't. I already knew your answer, so tonight we're celebrating on the beach. Party starts in an hour." As he pulled the door open they found Margery standing there. The alpha grunted something before moving past her, clearly giving them privacy.

Surprised by the mention of the party Rex stood as Margery entered.

She immediately smiled at him, taking his breath away—something she seemed to do at least once a day. "I love your manners," she murmured as she shut the door behind Grant.

Rex was from a different time, just like her, and not standing for a female simply wasn't done. He pulled her into his arms as he sat back against the chair, tugging her into his lap. She settled right over his growing erection, making him groan. "What else do you love about me?" he murmured, nipping at her jawline.

She wiggled over his hard length once, teasing him. "I'll tell you later. What did you guys talk about? Is there any news about the missing vamp?" The hope in her voice nearly shredded him.

She'd known he was coming up here to discuss hunting down Franz, and Rex had wanted to give her good news. "Nothing yet but we're going to find him. But, I do have good news. I'm joining the pack."

Her dark eyes widened before she kissed him, brushing her lips over his sweetly. "I can't believe you didn't tell me earlier, sneaky vampire," she said as she leaned back, her expression clearly pleased.

Not that he'd been worried she'd be disappointed. Okay, he'd been fucking nervous. What the hell was happening to him? It was like he'd turned into a lovesick fool. Shit. *He loved her.* That's why he felt overly protective and insecure. This had nothing to do with the electric pull he experienced because of what he knew was the mating call. This was different, deeper.

He loved her.

How had he not realized sooner? The past week they'd barely left her place. They'd had a lot of sex, but he'd also gotten to know her. He loved every single thing about her from the way she took care of so many of her packmates, just lending an ear to listen, right down to the way she sang horribly off-key in the shower.

Margery lightly thumped him on the chest and he realized he hadn't responded. "What are you thinking?"

"Living arrangements. I'll need to move all my stuff down here." Most of it was in a private, secure storage facility anyway because he traveled so much for work.

"The pack—*your* pack—will help. Will it be weird for you to be a vampire in a wolf pack?" Biting her bottom lip, she watched him curiously, and maybe a little nervously, as she waited for his answer.

"Hell no." He was certain he'd have to deal with the occasional challenges from pack members wanting to display dominance, but it would have been the same if he'd been in a coven. Supernatural beings were a lot more primal than humans in some ways.

She instantly relaxed, sliding her fingers over his shoulders. Even through his shirt the feel of her elegant fingers brushing against him turned him on even more. Because he'd been rock hard since he'd scented her out in the hallway. "We better get back to the condo. I don't think Grant would appreciate us going at it on his office floor."

The wicked gleam in her eyes told him that she was considering doing just that. Which made him even hotter. "I guess so." Sliding off him, she dragged her hand over his erection.

He groaned as he stood. "We're going to have to be quick. Grant's throwing a party in an hour."

"That's what he was talking about when he left? I didn't think he meant a real party," she said as he opened the door, heading out into the hallway first.

It was instinct for him to enter any space first to check for danger, even in their alpha's house.

"After you see how shifters party, you're never going to want to leave the pack," she continued, excitement lacing her voice.

He nearly snorted. He'd *never* leave. Not unless she did. And then he'd follow her anywhere. "Grant said there's an empty place next to yours I can take," he said abruptly. *But I don't want to stay there, I want to live with you,* he silently thought. Grant was right, he really was a coward.

"Oh...is that what you want?" she asked carefully. The shift in her scent was subtle as she stepped out behind him. It was sharper, one he'd never scented before, and he wasn't sure he liked it.

No, that wasn't what he wanted. He scrubbed a hand over his face as they paused outside the office door. He didn't want to live in another place. He wanted to be with Margery every second he could. If it was practically any other situation he could use his strength to get what he wanted. When hunting for someone he depended on strength, research and understanding the habits of his prey.

With Margery he felt impossibly out of his depth. This wasn't a game and while it was a hunt in a way, it wasn't one where there was one winner and one loser. He'd never been in a real relationship before and he couldn't screw this up. Not with her.

"Hey you two, break up whatever you're doing!" Talia shouted as she bounded up the stairs with Ella and Lauren Hayes, two jaguar shifters who had mated with Asher and Max, respectively, right on her heels. The two jaguars might as well be sisters for how much the petite, honey-blonde haired cousins looked like each other.

Right now the three women were practically jumping up and down with excitement. Lauren nudged him out of the way and grabbed Margery's hand. "Welcome to the pack, Rex," she said in his direction as she dragged Margery to the stairs. "We've got some party planning to do."

Margery smiled and shrugged as if to say 'what can you do' while Lauren dragged her away. Her smile was real but something lingered in her scent and in her expression that had those invisible icy fingers tightening around his throat again. Fuck, he was an idiot. He should just tell her he was moving in. Because he wasn't going anywhere.

* * *

At the tiki bar by the pool behind Grant's house, Margery grabbed another martini for herself and a beer for Rex. Rex didn't need to eat, but he could drink liquids other than blood. And she'd discovered that his favorite beer was *Dos Equis*. Grant must have known that too because he'd stocked the bar with them.

She was still impressed that Grant had managed to keep this party a secret from her. She was glad he had though because if Rex hadn't accepted joining the pack and she'd known about the party...She shook her head. No need to think about that because he was a member now, something that made her happier than she'd ever been. Even if he had mentioned moving into the empty place next to hers. She hadn't known how to respond and had been grateful when Lauren and the others had dragged her away to help prep for the party.

Maybe it was stupid but she'd assumed he'd move in with her. The last week had been amazing and more intense than she'd ever imagined possible. She knew what she felt for him and it was way more than the mating call. She'd thought he felt the same. Since she didn't want to depress herself, she locked all those thoughts down tight and made her way around the pool.

She ignored calls from her packmates to jump in and play volleyball and sidled up to Rex who was talking with Lauren and Max, Grant's second-in-command. He was one of her favorite packmates and she was so happy he'd found someone.

"You didn't have to get that," Rex murmured as he took the beer and wrapped his arm around her shoulders.

Even if she felt off-balance by what he'd said earlier, she loved how affectionate he was. There was no guessing where she stood as far as that went. "It's your party, you're not going to do anything but relax."

The heated look he gave her in response made her toes curl in her sandals. When a plastic beach ball flew past them, hitting Lauren in the head, the jaguar shifter playfully batted it back at a group of the partygoers and quickly excused herself to join them.

"Give us a few minutes?" Rex asked Max, who raised his eyebrows but trailed after his mate. Rex then took Margery's martini and set it on a nearby table next to his beer before taking her hand in his.

He linked his fingers through hers, his grip reassuring. "Take a walk with me."

"What about the party?" she asked as they headed down the private wooden boardwalk to the beach. Not that she really cared. She loved being alone with Rex.

Music was blasting, everyone was relaxed and drinking and she knew in an hour or so they'd move it to the beach for a bonfire. But for now it was just the two of them. There were a couple boats idling out in the water, the nearly full moon gleaming down on everything. He didn't respond until they reached the end of the long boardwalk. "What's going on with us?" His voice was so low she almost couldn't make out the question above the softly crashing waves in front of them and the party noise behind them.

"What do you mean?" He'd probably picked up on her emotions, something that was a good and bad thing. She gestured toward the surf, wanting to sit in the sand closer to the ocean. Even though that vampire was still out there, she and Rex were two strong supernatural beings. She wasn't worried about being ambushed. Especially not so close to the pack.

As they sat in the sand, he kept his fingers threaded through hers and he turned to face her. "Something's bothering you." A statement, not a question.

She sighed, knowing she needed to be honest. She might be new to this relationship stuff, but he deserved her honesty. Even if it would hurt if he told her that he didn't want to live with her. As she started to respond, her hair blew slightly back as something whistled past her face.

Rex threw his body over hers, tackling her against the soft sand. Something thudded behind them. An arrow. It took her less than a second to realize they were under attack.

"He's shooting from the water. Stay low," he ordered as he practically dragged her down the beach.

She shoved up from the sand and sprinted with him. A few thuds trailed after them, but none too close.

"You want to end this now?" Rex's eyes glowed intensely bright.

Without him having to explain what he wanted to do, she nodded. If that bastard out there thought he could hurt them on pack land, he was dumber than she thought. She heard the engine and knew they had only moments to make a decision. She stripped off her dress and shoes, leaving her in her bathing suit, as Rex slid his shoes and shirt off. Without a word, they both hurried toward the water, using their incredible speed to swim toward the boat.

It was starting to pull away, the shooter likely realizing the mistake he'd made. He might be good with a bow and arrow, but aiming from a moving boat had to be damn hard.

Rex pulled ahead of her, using his incredible speed as he cut through the water like a torpedo. The engine roared and panic jumped in her throat as the boat started to flee. She wanted this to end now, not wait for this asshole to come after them again.

Calling on all her strength, she stroked harder. Her fear blossomed into something sharp when she saw Rex jump from the water into the boat. As she reached the idling vessel, full-blown adrenaline took over. She clutched at the side and pulled herself up only to collapse in relief when she saw Rex standing next to a pile of ash already turning muddy as it mixed with the ocean water. She'd known he was strong, but damn.

Before she could swing herself over, Rex grabbed her under her arms and hauled her up, pulling her close. She shuddered at the sensations punching through her. He was safe, unharmed.

"It's over," Rex murmured. "Stupid fucker thought we had the money Stanley stole. He wanted it back."

Which meant the money was still out there. Not that Margery cared about that. She kept her arms wrapped tight around him as she leaned her head back to look up at Rex. She might be relationship challenged, but when it came to this male she had to tell him how she felt. If something had happened to him and she'd never gotten the chance it would have shredded her. He deserved to know this was more than just physical attraction and more than just the mating call. "I love you, Rex."

His eyes glowed brighter than she'd ever seen them, his expression dark, hungry and so full of love it made her knees weak. He wasn't holding anything back now. "I love you too, and I'm not moving into that empty, fucking condo. I'm moving in with you whether you like it or not."

She laughed at his almost angry declaration. "Good."

"Good?"

"Uh, yeah. I don't want to live without you." Even with her loving and supportive pack this week she realized that she'd been missing something. Rex was it.

"Thank God because I *can't* live without you. Hell, I can't believe I've lived hundreds of years without you. You make everything better, Margery. I sound like an idiot but around you everything is brighter and more beautiful." He looked almost bewildered as he spoke.

As if he couldn't believe he'd found her. She knew what he was feeling because she felt the exact same way.

She grabbed his face in her hands and tugged him down to her, needing to taste him. Their salt-slicked bodies molded to each other as their lips and tongues clashed in a fervent erotic mating. Something told her that as soon as they made it back to shore and got this mess straightened out, they'd be skipping the rest of the party and spending it back at her—their—place. That was more than fine with her. She wanted to seal their bond physically and have him drink from her again—claiming her in the most primal way.

EPILOGUE

Two months later

Rex's body tightened in anticipation when he heard the front door open, just as it did each time Margery walked into a room. The front door quietly closed and that sweet lavender scent made him go rock hard. He was like a trained monkey. All he had to do was smell her unique, erotic scent and he was ready to go.

"Hey, sweetheart," he called out from the living room. It was still daytime so the drapes and hurricane shutters were pulled tight, but the sun should be setting in less than an hour. And he had a date planned for them. They'd gone straight from sleeping together to living together and now he was making up for it, taking her out every chance he got. He'd also put an engagement ring on her finger.

He wanted every male, regardless of species, to know she was taken. She deserved the courting he'd planned to give her and he wanted marriage. He'd been human at one time and some dormant part of him needed to make the commitment even more official.

"Hey, babe." She strode into the room carrying a takeout bag of what he guessed was some of her favorite chocolate, buttercream cupcakes if the scent was any indication. She set the bag down on the coffee table along with her purse and keys.

He set his laptop on the cushion next to him and before he'd straightened she was straddling him. Her summer dress pushed up to her thighs, revealing beautiful, tan skin. "You're in a good mood."

"I don't have to work tonight, I have extra cupcakes that I don't have to worry about my mate stealing, and I've got the sexiest mate there is." Her smile was infectious as she raised up and slid her panty-covered mound over his unfortunately covered cock. That was about to change soon. "How's work going?" she murmured as she started working the buttons of his shirt free.

"Good," he rasped out, already unsteady at the thought of her hands all over him, of getting to kiss and touch her everywhere.

For the past couple months he'd been working on a new project, creating a private, intricate database for supernatural bounty hunters to information share, among other things. Right now work was the last thing on his mind though, especially when his mate's scent of pure lust was relentlessly teasing him.

As she slowly continued undressing him, his patience snapped, as it so often did when it came to Margery. Grabbing her hips, he stood and headed for the bedroom.

She giggled lightly, her hands moving to clutch onto his shoulders as he hurried. "It's going to be one of those nights, huh?"

"Definitely." Which was basically every night. He couldn't get enough of her. He'd thought this all-consuming lust for her would have faded a little, but it grew each time they were together, each time he pushed deep inside her and each time she gave him her blood.

As he laid her out on the bed they shared, his throat clenched with a no longer foreign emotion. He loved this female more than life itself and planned to show her every day for the rest of their lives.

Before her, he'd been a man caught between worlds, hunting his own kind and never fitting in with them. Never fitting in anywhere. Now he'd found a pack, friends, and more importantly the female he loved more than anything.

Thank you for reading Saving His Mate. I really hope you enjoyed it. If you don't want to miss any future releases, please feel free to join my newsletter. I only send out a newsletter for new releases or sales news. Find the signup link on my website: http://www.savannahstuartauthor.com

COMPLETE BOOKLIST

Miami Scorcher Series
Unleashed Temptation
Worth the Risk
Power Unleashed
Dangerous Craving
Desire Unleashed

Crescent Moon Series
Taming the Alpha
Claiming His Mate
Tempting His Mate
Saving His Mate

Futuristic Romance
Heated Mating
Claiming Her Warriors

Contemporary Erotic Romance
Adrianna's Cowboy
Tempting Alibi
Tempting Target
Tempting Trouble

ACKNOWLEDGMENTS

I owe a big thank you to Kari Walker and Carolyn Crane for reading early versions of this story. I'm also very grateful to Joan Turner for her input. And as always, I'm incredibly thankful to Tanya Hyatt who keeps me sane and helps out with so many behind the scenes things so I can spend more time writing! Last but never least, a huge thank you goes out to my readers! Thank you for buying my stories.

ABOUT THE AUTHOR

Savannah Stuart is the pseudonym of *New York Times* and *USA Today* bestselling author Katie Reus. Under this name she writes slightly hotter romance than her mainstream books. Her stories still have a touch of intrigue, suspense, or the paranormal and the one thing she always includes is a happy ending. She lives in the South with her very own real life hero. In addition to writing (and reading of course!) she loves traveling with her husband.

For more information about Savannah's books please visit her website at: www.savannahstuartauthor.com.

19315095R00082

Printed in Poland
by Amazon Fulfillment
Poland Sp. z o.o., Wrocław